ADVANCE PRAISE FOR *NONDISCLOSURE* BY GEOFFREY M. COOPER

"This book manages to accomplish, in a short space, what few books are capable of with far more pages. It is at once a compelling mystery, a fascinating peek into the politics of academia, and a nuanced look at the Me Too movement. This is a well-thought-out examination of current events and a worthy addition to the national conversation."
—Manhattan Book Review

"Geoffrey M. Cooper crafts a riveting saga of mystery, discovery, and redemption.... readers interested in medical thrillers will relish the turns taken in an engrossing story that's hard to put down."
—Midwest Book Review

"A fast-paced medical thriller with a cast full of brilliant characters. Engaging and suspenseful to the very end!"
—San Francisco Book Review

"Gene-targeted drugs and immunotherapy aren't normally the stuff of heady thrillers, but thanks to liberal doses of drama, deceit, and interpersonal relationships woven into the storyline, Nondisclosure *is a riveting read with wide appeal. A medical thriller with plenty of twists and turns,* Nondisclosure *is sure to satisfy lovers of the genre."*
—Self-Publishing Review

PRAISE FOR *THE PRIZE* BY GEOFFREY M. COOPER

"Fans of Robin Cook–style medical thrillers will relish the interpersonal relationships, drama, and contrast between lab and scientific research special interest...the result is a thoroughly engrossing science odyssey that touches upon social and research issues alike."

—Midwest Book Review

"An intense story about ruthlessness in the scientific community."

—Kirkus Reviews

"A fast-paced science thriller that would rival Michael Crichton or Patricia Cornwell."

—Manhattan Book Review

"Geoffrey M. Cooper creates stunning antagonists in The Prize, *while peeling back the curtain of the scientific community to reveal its humanity. A great read for science lovers and anyone who enjoys a big, juicy scandal."*

—IndieReader

"The Prize is a clever, suspenseful page-turner for seasoned lab-coat wearers and novice geeks alike."

—Colorado Book Review

"A medical thriller at its best . . . a page-turner that is intelligently plotted and accomplished with unusual finesse and mastery."

—Readers' Favorite

"What Geoffrey Cooper, a former professor and cancer researcher, has produced here is an engaging and page-turning thriller with a scientific context."

—Popular Science

"[A] serious account of how scientific investigation can be side-tracked by chicanery. . . . The end spirals to a climax that is only partially predictable."

—San Francisco Book Review

NONDISCLOSURE

NONDISCLOSURE

A
MEDICAL
THRILLER

GEOFFREY M. COOPER

Grateful acknowledgment is made to the National Academies Press for permission to reprint an excerpt from *Sexual Harassment of Women: Climate, Culture, and Consequences in Academic Sciences, Engineering, and Medicine*, Paula Johnson and Sheila Widnall, 2018. Permission conveyed through Copyright Clearance Center, Inc.

ISBN 978-1-7337714-0-5 (paperback)
ISBN 978-1-7337714-1-2 (ebook)

Cover and interior design by Lance Buckley.
www.lancebuckley.com

"Through our work it became clear that sexual harassment is a serious issue for women at all levels in academic science, engineering, and medicine, and that these fields share characteristics that create conditions that make harassment more likely to occur."

—Paula A. Johnson and Sheila Widnall, Cochairs, Committee on the Impacts of Sexual Harassment in Academia*

*National Academies of Sciences, Engineering, and Medicine. *Sexual Harassment of Women: Climate, Culture, and Consequences in Academic Sciences, Engineering, and Medicine.* Washington, DC: The National Academies Press, 2018.

1

I reached behind me to get the box of tissues I kept in my office for visitors. Usually they were needed by students who were meeting with me because they were having trouble with one of their professors and hoped that the chair of the department could smooth things over. But today was different. Kristy was my administrative assistant, not a student. She was probably the best I'd worked with in my twenty-odd years as a faculty member, normally cool and super-competent. But right now, she was close to tears, and there didn't seem to be a damn thing I could do for her. Especially with only half an hour left to go before our annual meeting with the dean.

"C'mon, it's not such a big deal," I offered, hoping to at least calm her down.

She looked up from the stack of files spread out in front of her on my conference table. "How can you say that? We're about to go to the dean's office for our annual budget meeting, and we're missing almost twenty thousand dollars in department discretionary funds. They'll tear us apart."

"They'll fuss a bit, sure. But we're a productive department at one of Boston's top research universities. Twenty thousand is a drop in the bucket—less than one percent of the request I've made for new department facilities. We've got to keep focused on the big picture. I know you don't like the fact that you can't account for every dollar, but the dean isn't going to care."

"Maybe not. But it's my twenty thousand, and that jerk Carlson is going to ream me out. Not only that, he's the one who has to sign off on my annual raise. I may have to sleep with the asshole to make up for this."

She forced a smile as she said it, but I knew she wasn't completely joking. Carlson was the college's chief financial officer. He enjoyed making people squirm, and I'd heard the other rumors too. I tried to be reassuring. "Look, I'll handle Carlson. Your girlfriend wouldn't like it if you had to sleep with him."

She almost laughed. Good, more like her usual self. "No, Nancy wouldn't like it." She shook her head. "Let's keep looking. We still have some time before the meeting."

She picked up the next file and started flipping pages when a hammering at the door startled us both. An unexpected interruption. People usually took a closed door to my office as a sign to go away.

I frowned. "Guess we better see who the hell that is."

"Okay, I'll get it."

I watched as she walked across my office. She'd dressed in a smart-looking gray business suit for our meeting. Professional, yet attractive. I could see why she thought Carlson might hit on her. Made me think that I should be wearing something other than chinos and my well-worn corduroy jacket. But I was still an academic, even though I was now chair of the Department of Integrated Life Sciences. I didn't have to dress like a businessman.

Kristy opened the door and said, "I'm sorry, we're tied up preparing for our finance meeting with the dean. Can I book an appointment for you tomorrow?"

Mike Singer's husky voice was unmistakable. "No, this can't wait. I really need to see Brad right away."

Singer wasn't someone to be trifled with. He was one of our star researchers—the best-funded member of my department and a frequently mentioned candidate for a Nobel Prize. He also seemed to have a direct line to the president of the university, which he was happy to use to go over my head when he wanted something.

"It's okay, Kristy," I said. "Let me talk to Mike for a few minutes. You can keep going through the papers."

I got up from the conference table to greet him. Kristy grabbed the stack of folders and took them to her desk in the outer office as Singer lumbered across the room and took her place. His neatly trimmed black beard and imposing figure—I put him at around six foot two and 220 pounds—fit the image of someone who was used to being in charge. I was no lightweight, but the couple of extra inches and twenty pounds he had on me made me feel diminutive in his presence.

"What's up, Mike?" I asked. "You know my door's always open to you, but things are a little hectic right now, getting ready for our annual budget meeting."

"I understand, but this is an emergency. A student's been attacked."

I sat up straight in my chair. "What do you mean? What's going on?"

"It's one of the graduate students, Emily Jackson. She's been assaulted, maybe even raped."

That brought me to full alert. "By who? She's not one of your students, is she?"

"No, she's Steve's student. And I think he's the one."

"Steve Upton?" That was tough to believe. Upton was mild-mannered and popular with students and faculty alike. Not someone I'd suspect of sexual misconduct, or worse. But you could never tell.

"Yes, Steve Upton," Singer spat out. "My closest collaborator, damn it. And this is really going to screw up our research. As you know, we're onto something big, and having Steve involved in a sexual assault case is going to be a mess. But whatever the fallout, I can't ignore what he's done. The girl, Emily, sent a text to one of my students this morning. Here's a printout. See for yourself."

He handed me a screenshot of the text. I read it twice, stalling for time as I tried to get my head around it.

Carol, I'm at the airport. I've got to get out of here. Something happened last night, I don't even know what. But this morning I woke up on the couch half-naked with my pants pulled down around my ankles. I remember someone doing things to me, but I don't know who or what or why I let him. Or even if I did. It's just too awful, and I can't face anyone in the lab. I'm going home to Chicago. I'm not sure for how long, but I'll let you know when I'm coming back to Boston. Don't tell anyone, please!

"Hang on a minute, Mike." I got up and grabbed a notepad from my desk. I wanted to get the details straight for my meeting with the dean. Like it or not, this was going to usurp whatever else we had on the agenda.

"Okay, let's go through this, so I can get it right. I take it that Carol is your student? And presumably a friend of Emily's?"

Singer nodded. "Yes, the two of them are close friends. They're the two leads on the big collaborative project Steve and I have been working on. Emily's his student, and Carol's mine. Together, they've put together a story that's going to revolutionize the field."

"I know. You've told us about their work. But let's focus on this text for now."

The last thing I needed at the moment was another exposition on Mike Singer's science. I'd had the dubious privilege of listening to him toot his own horn often enough. "Why would Emily have sent this to Carol instead of reporting whatever happened to me or the college office that handles sexual harassment?" I asked. "And for that matter, why did Carol take it to you?"

"Didn't you read the text?" He addressed me, as usual, like I was the village idiot. But I'd learned not to take offense—it was the way he felt about everybody. His arrogance was a pain in the ass, but he wasn't much different in that regard from many accomplished scientists at leading universities. It seemed to come with the territory.

"Emily didn't want to talk about it, and she specifically asked Carol not to tell anyone either. All Emily wanted to do was to get away, but she had to let her best friend and colleague know what was going on. When Emily didn't show up for our regular weekly meeting this afternoon, I asked Carol where she was. Carol felt bad betraying her confidence, but I pressed her, and she eventually broke down and showed me the text."

"Okay, but what about Steve Upton? Why are you suggesting it was him, whatever happened?"

"Because I was out with him and the girls last night, the bastard. Emily had too much to drink, and he took her home."

"Wait a minute, what do you mean—the four of you went out last night?" I glared at him with my accusing department chair expression. "You're not dating your students, are you?"

He gave me his "what a jerk you are" look. "No, of course not. Our paper just got accepted yesterday by *Nature*. It'll blow the whole field open by showing how effectively we can treat lung cancer with a combination of a new gene-targeted drug and immunotherapy. Emily and Carol are the two first authors, so Steve and I took them out for a nice dinner to celebrate."

I scribbled furiously. "Okay, fine. Having your students land a paper in the world's most prestigious journal is certainly worth celebrating. What happened?"

"We went to the Mexican restaurant in Back Bay—you know, where we usually take department visitors."

I nodded. "El Camino?"

"Right. We had their melted cheese appetizer and got a platter of enchiladas for the table. And a couple of pitchers of margaritas. I guess Emily had too much to drink, and by the end of dinner, she was pretty tipsy."

Great, two of my top faculty members going out with their students and getting them drunk. Special occasion or not, this would look just super in the *Boston Globe*.

I shook my head. "Do you know how stupid that sounds?"

He shrugged. "Look, it was just an innocent celebration. Or at least I thought so. Anyway, by the time we were ready to leave, Emily was too zonked to walk straight, so I put everyone in my car to take her home. Carol lives just a couple of blocks from the restaurant, so we dropped her off, and then we drove to Emily's apartment in Brookline. Steve got out with her and helped her upstairs to her place on the second floor. I saw the lights go on for a few minutes, then off again, and he came back to the car. Said he'd gotten her onto her couch, and she was passed out. Then I drove him back to where his car was parked near the lab, and that was it. I went up to my office to get some things off my desk and then went home."

"What are you saying? You think he had sex with her when he was up in her apartment?"

"What else is there to think? He was alone with her, and she passed out. And he was pretty loaded too. I think he couldn't resist pulling down her pants and doing, well, whatever he did. The bastard."

"How long was he in the apartment with her?" I asked.

"Maybe ten minutes or so. Long enough."

I looked up at the ceiling. "I guess it's possible, but it's hard to believe Steve would do something like that."

"What else could have happened?"

"I don't know. Maybe someone else found her passed out on the couch later. A boyfriend? I just don't want to put the blame on Steve too quickly."

Singer shook his head. "I don't think so. Steve's always playing around with his students. Emily's one of his favorites, and he's probably been trying to get in her pants for months. Last night he had the perfect opportunity. I wouldn't be surprised if he even put something in her drink at dinner."

I sighed. What a mess. At least my meeting with the dean was well timed. I could tell her what I knew, and she'd have the right people take over.

"Okay, Mike. Thank you for bringing this to me so promptly." I stood up to signal the end of our meeting. "Emily's in Chicago now and out of harm's way, right?"

"Yeah, she's okay for now."

"All right, then. We have our annual budget meeting in fifteen minutes, and I'll take the opportunity to brief the dean on this. I suspect the procedure will be to initiate an investigation from the college sexual harassment office, and they'll no doubt be in touch with you shortly. In the meantime, don't say anything to Steve, okay?"

"I don't intend to ever speak to that son of a bitch again."

He got up and left, and I followed him across the office to get my coat. It was time to head over to our meeting with the dean. There was suddenly a lot more on the docket than I'd planned.

2

Rain was falling as Kristy and I walked across campus to the college administration building. The whole summer had been like this, hot and rainy, and it was continuing through the fall. I had my raincoat, but Kristy also had an umbrella and insisted on trying to share it with me, despite my protests. As a result, we made slow progress, and both of us got wet.

Kristy was uncharacteristically quiet, I assumed still worrying about the missing twenty thousand. That was fine with me. My head was spinning with the implications of a messy sexual misconduct case—okay, maybe rape—involving one of the top researchers in my department. If Upton was guilty of assaulting a student, his dismissal would be a foregone conclusion. And well deserved. But I also had to think about how to protect the department from collateral damage by the publicity that would follow. And the implications of shutting down Upton's lab, with the necessity of finding new positions for the dozen or so junior researchers—graduate students and research associates—that he currently supported. The damage he'd done not only to Emily but to the entire department, especially his other students, was incalculable. Kristy's missing twenty thousand paled in comparison.

By the time we reached the administration building, we were late as well as wet, and it was a few minutes after five thirty by the time we took the elevator up to the dean's office on the fourth floor. An administrative assistant was watching for us and ushered us into the inner office, where the dean was waiting at the head of her conference table. Claire Houghton was an accomplished economist who'd spent the last fifteen or so years moving through the upper levels of university administration. Now in her early fifties, she was a master of academic politics and bore the mantle of her office as comfortably as she wore her navy blue business suit and gold tassel necklace. Ed Carlson, the college chief financial officer, sat on her right. Partially balding, with a thin face and long, hooked nose, he kept staring at the papers in front of him without acknowledging our presence—the image of an IRS examiner ready to conduct an audit.

The office made mine feel cramped, and it seemed as if it took several minutes for Kristy and me to follow the administrative assistant across an oversize oriental rug to the conference table. We sat on the opposite side from Carlson, and the admin took a seat at the end of the table.

The dean began by pointing out the obvious. "You're late, and we don't have much time. I have another meeting at six fifteen."

"I'm sorry," I said. "Unfortunately, there's an emergency situation that just arose, and I'm going to need some time to talk to you about that in addition to our discussion of the budget."

"What's that supposed to mean? What kind of emergency?"

"It's serious, but I don't think we should talk about it in front of the others. We need to save ten minutes at the end to deal with it."

She frowned to show me that she didn't like having her meeting hijacked. But she knew me well enough to take what I said seriously. "All right, then, let's get on with it." She looked at her notes. "Your major budget request is close to three million dollars for equipment and renovations to develop a new facility in your department for proteomics, which I understand is the large-scale analysis of the proteins that are expressed by different kinds of cells." She glanced down again at the paper in front of her. "You talk about a number of applications, like looking for differences between cancer cells and normal cells to find new targets for cancer therapy. That all sounds fine, but you're asking for a heavy chunk of change. How will this new toy—a mass spectrometer, you call it—really benefit your department? After all, you science guys have already sequenced the whole human genome. Doesn't that give you everything you need?"

I started into my planned justification. This was science, ground I was comfortable with. And although the dean wasn't a scientist, I knew she was an intelligent listener. "This technology, proteomics, gives us a lot more information than just the DNA sequence of the genome. You can think of the genome sequence as a blueprint. It has the plans for all of the possible things that a cell can do. But what a cell *actually does* is determined by which of the twenty thousand or so genes in the genome are expressed at a particular time. It's differences in gene expression that make a liver cell different from a muscle cell, or a cancer cell different from a normal cell. And that's what proteomics measures—differences in gene expression, not just the genes themselves."

She pursed her lips and nodded. "Okay, got it. And who in the department would make use of this?"

"Quite a few of our faculty. Probably Mike Singer would be the biggest user. Fisher, Clements, and Dworkin would be others. My own lab would use it too." Steve Upton would be another heavy user, but I wasn't going to mention him, given what was to come.

The dean pulled another piece of paper out of her file. "Mike Singer, huh? I guess that explains why I've already heard from the president, saying that he's strongly supportive and will contribute to funding your request. Singer must've pulled one of his usual end arounds and gone over my head. Did you know about that?"

I sighed and shook my head. "No, of course I didn't know. You know that I respect your place in the chain of command. But I can't say I'm surprised that Singer went over both of us."

She shrugged. "Oh well, I guess that means you get your new toy. Congratulations on an easy three million. Courtesy of Mike Singer and *El Presidenté*."

I didn't like the fact that Singer had end-run me, but in this case, it was for a good cause. And he'd succeeded on behalf of the department, so who was I to complain?

I started to thank the dean, but she held up a hand. "Let's move on and give ourselves time to deal with your emergency." Looking over at Carlson, she asked, "What else do we need to discuss?"

Carlson's mouth was tightly drawn. "They're trying to hood-wink us with their annual report. There's some twenty thousand dollars unaccounted for in their discretionary expenditures from last year, and I suspect all this rush is just a ruse to avoid our looking into it."

"No, I'm afraid the rush is real enough," I said. "There's no need to be hostile."

Kristy spoke up. "I know. I noticed the discrepancy too. I just saw it a couple of days ago, after we submitted our report, and I was hoping to have it tracked down by the time we met today."

"And do you?" Carlson asked.

"I'm sorry, but I haven't been able to figure it out yet. I think it's buried somewhere in travel receipts. Don't worry—I'll keep working on it and get it straightened out."

Carlson looked down his nose and snorted. "It should have been straightened out before you submitted your report, let alone came to this meeting. We don't have time to deal with nonsense like this in here. And we wouldn't have to if you did your job the way it should be done."

Kristy paled, and I jumped in. "You're being abusive, Carlson, and that's uncalled for. She said we'll figure it out, and we will. But twenty thousand dollars is peanuts in a major research university. Maybe you should get some perspective on what we're doing here. We're BTI, the Boston Technological Institute. Maybe we're not in the same league as our Cambridge buddies across the river –Harvard and MIT—but we're not some mom-and-pop liquor store either."

The dean interrupted before he could answer. "All right, guys, stop it. We don't do abusive here." She gave Carlson a hard look. "I'd like you to work with Kristy to figure this out. And if there's nothing else, please give Brad and me the room."

When the others had left, she said, "Sorry about that. He can be an ass, but he's good with numbers. Now, what's up?"

"Mike Singer barged into my office just before this meeting, accusing Steve Upton of sexually assaulting one of his students."

Her eyes widened. "Jesus! No wonder you wanted to get this on our agenda." She picked up her notepad. "Okay, tell me."

I took her through Singer's story. When I finished, she sat there for a minute, shaking her head. When she finally spoke, the look on her face was somewhere between sad and angry.

"Unbelievable. How could anyone be such a bastard? Sounds to me like Upton drugged the student's drink at dinner, planning all the time to take her back to her apartment and assault her. Is that your take on it?"

"Yes, I'm afraid that's what it sounds like. Although so far, we only have a third-person account from Singer. We need to hear what the student has to say and also give Upton a chance to tell his side of the story."

"Of course, but it seems clear enough. And we're past the days when a big shot like Upton can explain something like this away as 'he says, she says.' You've heard of Me Too, right? I want the bastard's head."

"If he's guilty, I don't disagree. But I do have trouble believing that Steve Upton would do this. We just need to follow through on Singer's story and make sure we have all the facts."

She leaned back and nodded. "Of course. We need to investigate thoroughly and close any loopholes. I'm going to give this case to Karen Richmond. She's our top investigator for handling Title IX complaints—everything involving sexual misconduct. Sharp as a tack. I think you'll like working with her."

Working with her? That gave me a start. "What do you mean working with her? I'll tell her my story, sure, but after that, I assume she'll take over, no?"

The dean gave a sarcastic snort. "You wish. No, I'm afraid we need you to play an active role in the investigation. It's your department, and you know the people involved, both faculty and students. You're going to have to work with Karen as her guide and coinvestigator while she plows her way through this. Given the stature of the accused—one of your top faculty members— the investigation has to be airtight and leave no room for any complaints afterward. So your job is to work hand in hand with

Karen to be sure she gets all the information she needs. And that Upton gets his day in court, so he can't say he was railroaded."

"Look, I'm a scientist, not a criminal investigator. This isn't something I know how to do."

"You're also department chair, Brad. And this falls solidly within your job description, whether you like it or not. Am I being clear?"

I groaned inwardly but gave her a mock salute. Fortunately, we liked each other. "Okay, boss. Got it."

She snickered as I got up and left the office. On my way out, I ran into the group already assembled for her next meeting. It included Carlson, who glared daggers at me.

———

I went back to the office to finish clearing my desk for the day and then walked home to my condo in Back Bay. It was a renovated Victorian in a three-story, 1870s brownstone on Commonwealth Avenue, just over a mile from my office, with plenty of stores and restaurants nearby. I took advantage of the location tonight by stopping at Capellini's to pick up a meatball sub for an easy dinner—I was too preoccupied to cook.

Despite the unease I felt about dealing with Upton's case, my mood lightened when I was greeted at the door by an excited Rosie, jumping up and down and spinning in circles. Who could resist twenty pounds of unadulterated exuberance?

I'd adopted her a couple of years ago, when I was dating a vet. Sarah brought the six-month-old pug puppy over to visit after she'd been surrendered to the clinic because her owner had suffered a stroke and could no longer take care of her. Sarah was convinced I needed a dog, and I didn't disagree, being a longtime dog lover. The pup clinched the deal when I picked her up and she fell asleep happily in my arms, head on my shoulder. I named her Rosie, after Rosalind Franklin, the woman who'd done the experiments that Watson and Crick used to determine their famous structure of DNA in 1953. Watson and Crick received a Nobel Prize, whereas Franklin's contribution was never properly recognized, so I made sure that Rosie received plenty of love and attention to compensate for her namesake's neglect.

We had a welcome-home cuddle, and Rosie followed me into the kitchen to get our evening treats. A beef jerky strip for her and a single-malt scotch for me. A note from Ellen, my twelve-year-old downstairs neighbor who took care of Rosie while I was out, was in its usual place on the kitchen counter, next to the bottle of scotch. She'd fed and walked Rosie around five, so Rosie was all set for a while. Ellen was a tremendous boon. She loved Rosie as much as I did and was thrilled to take care of her during the day. And just as happy to keep her downstairs overnight when I was traveling.

I took my drink and sandwich over to the overstuffed chair in the living room, next to a window overlooking the mall, the tree-lined park in the middle of Commonwealth Avenue that ran through the city to the Public Garden. Rosie's jerky strip was long since gone, but she was happy to jump into my lap and watch the people and dogs on the mall while I had my drink and dinner.

The combination of Rosie, food, and good scotch helped smooth out the day's wrinkles. But I was still far from comfortable with all that had gone on. My new assignment seemed like another clash of my career with the Peter Principle—the dubious management approach of promoting people until they reach a position at which they are no longer competent.

At an earlier stage of my professional life, I'd made my share of important discoveries in the field of cancer genetics. Those discoveries had been rewarded with a promotion to tenured professor, substantial grants for my research, invitations to deliver prestigious lectures, and other kinds of recognition bestowed on successful scientists.

Then Dean Houghton screwed it all up by asking me to take on the position of department chair. I resisted at first, but the previous chair had been unceremoniously dismissed for hijacking department funds to support his own research, and several of my colleagues in the department urged me to accept, arguing that there weren't any other plausible candidates. So at the age of forty-six, I accepted a position of major administrative responsibility. A job for which I had no qualifications, no training, and no experience. Not to mention, no desire.

I guess I did okay, at least compared with the previous occupant of the office. But the administration and politics associated with being chair took me away from my research, leaving me without enough time to do what I *was* good at. And now I was going to add to this burden by taking on a sexual assault investigation.

Still, I hated what had happened to Emily. If they needed me to help bring Steve Upton down for this, I'd step up. And try to protect the integrity of the science and the morale of the department in the process.

Besides, it should be quick and easy. A couple of interviews with this investigator woman should do the trick. Talk to Emily, Carol, maybe Singer again. Then give Upton a chance to say his piece, and it would all be done. No reason to sweat it.

3

The office had an appealing smell of fresh coffee when I got in around eight fifteen the next morning. Kristy was at her desk in the outer office with a pastry box open in front of her. Raspberry scones from Yeast and Flour, a bakery near her house in Harvard Square.

"What's the occasion?" I asked.

"A little thank-you for the way you stood up to that jerk Carlson yesterday."

I smiled at her. "No big deal. My pleasure, in fact." I took a scone. "But I'm happy to accept one of these as a reward."

"You better hurry and enjoy them. Your visitor is already on her second one."

"Visitor?" I looked around the corner into the waiting room and saw a woman sitting on the couch, balancing a scone and coffee with her iPad. "Who is she?"

"I'm sorry. She said you were expecting her. Karen Richmond from Dean Houghton's office. She was here at eight when I got in, and she's been munching on scones and coffee ever since."

"Guess she skipped breakfast to get here early. Yes, I am expecting her. Just wasn't ready quite yet."

I went out to the waiting room and said, "Hi, I'm Brad Parker."

She got up from the couch, putting her iPad down to offer her hand. A slim blonde, maybe forty or so, dressed in a light, blue-and-white striped blouse and dark blue slacks. "I'm Karen Richmond. Nice to meet you." She grinned and held up a half-eaten scone. "And thanks for your morning hospitality."

"No problem. A little reward from my administrative assistant for being a good boy yesterday." She looked at me quizzically, but I didn't bother explaining. Instead I said, "C'mon in and let's talk."

I led her into my office and sat behind my desk, motioning her to one of the visitor chairs across from me. "I wasn't expecting you quite so soon."

She shrugged. "The dean called last night and filled me in. I figured why wait. Maybe I could catch you early. This is clearly a matter we want to deal with as quickly as possible."

"I agree. The sooner we can clear this up, the better. I'll free up whatever time you need."

"Good, thank you. If you don't mind, let's start by having you tell me about your meeting with Mike Singer. The dean briefed me, but I'd like to hear the story directly from you." She took out a cell phone. "You don't mind if I record it, do you?"

"Of course not." I got my notes and took her through what I knew.

When I finished, she nodded and said, "Right, that's pretty much what the dean told me. Sounds awful, but as she said you already pointed out, it's all thirdhand at this point. We have some work ahead of us."

"Where do you want to start?" I asked. "Should I get Singer in here so you can talk to him directly?"

"Not yet. I'll want to talk to him later, but before that, I'd like to get a firsthand account from the victim. Emily."

"She's in Chicago now."

"I know. We'll have to make a trip out there to interview her. These things are really done much better in person than over the phone. Are you free to get away in the next couple of days?"

"Both of us need to go?" I asked. She certainly moved fast.

"Yes, I'm afraid so. I want someone besides myself at all of these interviews, and I need your background knowledge of the people involved to work effectively." She smiled. "So we're going to be joined at the hip until we figure this out. Can you handle it?"

I returned the smile. She seemed pleasant enough, as well as efficient. Maybe working with her wouldn't be so bad. "What happened to Emily is intolerable," I said. "I'll do whatever you need to help."

"Thank you. I appreciate your cooperation. The question now is how to approach Emily. I don't think we should just fly out there cold. We need to call her first and tell her we'd like to come out and talk to her."

"That sounds right," I said. "I'm sure we have her phone number on file. I'll ask Kristy to get it."

"I already have it." She handed me a piece of paper. Efficient for sure.

Then she surprised me. "I think you should make the call. Just tell her that you heard what happened, and you're very sorry. Her text suggests that she's terribly upset, so you need to be as comforting and reassuring as possible. Put me on speaker, and you can introduce me as a representative from the dean's office who deals with these cases. Then see if we can set a time to meet with her tomorrow."

"Why me? You know what to say. Shouldn't you be the one to call her? Or I can get her on the phone and then turn it over to you."

She shook her head. "No, that's why I need you working with me on this. She knows you—at least as the chair of her department if not personally. Either way, she's going to be far more comfortable talking with you than with me, a total stranger. Sorry, but this one falls in your court."

I sighed. "Okay, got it." I started to pick up the phone when something else occurred to me. "How do I explain what I know to her? I mean, do I tell her about Singer coming to me with the text? She asked her friend Carol not to share it with anyone, so it seems like I'm breaking a confidence if I tell her what happened."

Karen took a minute to consider that. "You're right. We should try to keep Carol's name out of it. If she asks, I think you have to say that you heard about it secondhand, but you can't reveal the source because of confidentiality. If you present us as concerned and sympathetic, she may just be grateful that someone in a position of authority is willing to step up and help, without caring about how you found out."

I was dubious. After all, she hadn't come forward to get help and had told Carol not to tell anyone. But Karen was the expert. "Okay," I said. "Here goes."

I placed the call, and she picked up on the second ring. "Hi, this is Emily." Her voice was strong and confident.

"Hi Emily, this is Brad Parker."

"Oh, Professor Parker!" She giggled. "You surprised me by saying 'Brad.' What's up? Is there some kind of problem?"

This didn't sound like a victim of assault. I raised an eyebrow and looked at Karen, but she shrugged and motioned that I should go ahead. So I did.

"Emily, I first want to say how very, very sorry I am for what happened to you Tuesday night. Most important, I want to see if you're doing okay. And I want to assure you that we're going to do everything possible to bring whoever hurt you to justice and make sure he never harms another student. I have Karen Richmond from the dean's office with us on speakerphone. She's an expert at handling sexual assault cases and will be working with me to help you."

Karen gave me a thumbs-up. So far, so good.

Then Emily said, "What in the world are you talking about? Have you called the right person?"

I looked up in shock. This was the last thing I'd expected. Karen's open-mouthed stare suggested a similar reaction.

I gathered my wits and used my most soothing voice. "I understand why you didn't want to tell anyone, believe me. Something as horrible as what happened to you, sometimes we just want to keep things like that to ourselves and bottle them up. But it doesn't work. It just keeps festering inside. Please let us help you."

Karen jumped in and said, "Professor Parker's right, Emily. I've dealt with a lot of cases like this, and I can promise that you'll feel much better after you talk to us."

"Guys, that's all really nice of you, but I don't know what you're talking about. Nothing has happened to me. I'm just here in Chicago to help my mom for a few days. She's in the hospital after falling down some stairs. But she's okay, and I'll be back in the lab on Monday."

Karen said, "You went out to dinner Tuesday night with another student and two of your professors, right?"

"That's right. The professors took us out to celebrate our paper getting accepted. It's going to be in *Nature*, so it's a big deal."

"And the next morning, you sent a text to your friend saying that you couldn't remember what happened, but you woke up on the couch with your clothes off."

Silence. "I guess you saw my text. I'm sorry—I was just trying to spoof Carol a bit. She's always such a busybody. Really, nothing happened."

Karen sighed. "Well, I'm glad you're all right. But since allegations have been made, we still need to investigate. Professor Parker and I would like to fly out to Chicago tomorrow to talk with you. Is there a good time for you to meet?"

Now Emily sounded annoyed. "For Pete's sake, let it go! How many times do I have to tell you nothing happened? I just have a couple of days here with my mom, and I don't want to waste time on this. I'll talk to you when I get back to Boston, if I have to." She hung up.

I put down the phone and looked at Karen. She looked as baffled as I felt.

"What the hell do you make of that?" I asked.

"I don't know," she said. "Something's really weird. Her text didn't sound like a joke to me, and Singer obviously took it seriously. As did her friend Carol."

"Obviously. But if she wanted to play a trick on them, she succeeded."

"It's possible," Karen said. "Although it'd be a pretty crappy trick. Alternatively, though, maybe she's afraid of pursuing accusations against her advisor. After all, Upton has essentially complete power over her, doesn't he?"

"For better or worse, that's how science education works, especially for graduate students," I said. "But that doesn't mean she has to let him get away with harassment or assault. We can help her with that."

Karen nodded. "We can indeed, but only if she pulls together enough courage to talk to us. In any case, we need to get to the bottom of this. Can you have your assistant get her in to meet with us on Monday? I want to see her in person."

"Sure," I said. "In the meantime, do you think we should go ahead and talk to Singer and Carol? See what they have to say about Emily's response?"

"Yes, I'd like to hear their reactions. See if you can set up times for us to meet with them later today or tomorrow. Let's talk to Singer first and then Carol. I'll make myself available whenever you can get them in here. If Emily's text was a joke, we need to have a serious talk with her about inappropriate behavior. But more likely, I think it's real, and she's reluctant to bring charges. Which I'm afraid is pretty common among victims of sexual assault. We're just going to have to work a little harder to get her to talk to us."

4

Kristy was able to get Singer scheduled for two that afternoon, with his student Carol then coming in at four. My new coinvestigator was available, so our next step was in place, and I was free to attend the weekly department seminar at noon. All of the graduate students presented a seminar on their work annually, and by a happy coincidence, Carol was on today. It'd be a good chance for me to get updated on the research before becoming immersed in trying to get to the bottom of the assault charges. After all, I reminded myself, protecting the integrity of the research was one of the things I wanted to accomplish in this investigation.

Seminars were held in the first-floor lecture hall of our new Interdisciplinary Research Building, a block down from my chair's office, which was in an older and grungier building that housed classrooms and the department administrative offices. I left ten minutes early and stopped by one of my favorite lunch trucks to pick up a grilled lamb gyro and a Diet Coke. It was just noon when I got to the auditorium and took a seat near the back. There was a good crowd. The 110-seat room was about two-thirds filled with department faculty and students. Singer was sitting in the front row, next to Carol, ready to perform the ritual of introducing his student to the audience. Steve Upton was there, too, sitting three rows back. All the players except one—our victim. If that's what Emily was.

At two minutes after twelve, Singer strode to the podium. He introduced Carol as a fourth-year student who was one of the most outstanding young researchers he'd had the pleasure of working with. He described the work she'd be presenting as the results of a close collaboration with his colleague Steve Upton and Steve's student Emily Jackson, noting that their paper had just been accepted by *Nature*, needing just a couple of minor tweaks to finish up. Then he led a round of welcoming applause for Carol as she took her place at the podium.

Most students were visibly nervous at the start of their presentations, but not Carol. Seeming as calm and smooth as if she'd done this for years, she thanked Professor Singer for all his support and launched into her story. She gave an excellent talk, polished and professional. First, she described the successes and limitations of what had become the two most promising new approaches to cancer treatment—gene-targeted drugs and immunotherapy. They both worked, sometimes dramatically. But in most cases, they were only effective for a fraction of patients and often worked for only a few months before cancers became resistant and no longer responded to treatment.

Carol explained that the idea behind her work was to combine these two approaches and hit cancers with a double whammy. She and her collaborator, Emily Jackson, had developed a drug cocktail that specifically made cancer cells more sensitive to attack by the immune system. Then she started showing the results of their experiments. In three different kinds of mouse cancer models, the combination of immunotherapy and their drug cocktail—*Immunoboost,* they called it—completely eradicated the cancer. The response compared with the partial effect of immunotherapy alone was striking.

This would be a spectacular advance if it worked in people. And they were going to find out. Carol concluded her talk by explaining that the work was patented and that they were in negotiations with one of the major pharmaceutical companies to begin clinical trials. The drugs in the cocktail were already approved for human use, and rapid progress to the clinic was possible.

The audience responded with loud and lengthy applause. And it was well deserved. No question that this was big—maybe a major breakthrough. Nobel Prize stuff with the potential of helping a lot of people.

Whatever the outcome of the sexual assault case, I couldn't let it tarnish these findings.

———

A couple of faculty members grabbed me to talk after the lecture, and it was one forty-five when I got back to my office. Karen was already there, ready for our planned pre-meeting before interviewing Mike Singer, sitting in the waiting room, nibbling on another scone.

"Do you just come here for the scones?" I asked. "I'm not sure they contain all the nutritional stuff you're supposed to eat."

She smiled. "They're good. And they have raspberries in them, right? What more could a girl need. Besides, I didn't have time for lunch."

"Oh, another urgent case?"

"You don't want to know. And I couldn't tell you anyway." She got up from the couch. "Ready to plan our next meeting?"

I led her into my office and sat down at my desk. But she shook her head and went over to the conference table. "I think we should sit here to give these interviews a clear sense of formality," she said. "You sit at the head of the table, I'll sit at your right, and we'll have the subject sit across from me. We can record on my phone, which I'll put in the center, and we'll both take notes."

I raised an eyebrow. "Glad to see you have this planned out. One might think you've done it before."

She ignored my levity. "It's important to set things up right. We're not here to have a pleasant chat with these folks. We want them to know that it's a serious interrogation, and what they say is on the record."

"Got it. Do you want to lead off?"

"No," she said. "You take the lead and introduce me as a representative from the dean's office, like you did on the phone with Emily. Get them talking, and I'll chime in as necessary. With Singer, I think you want to tell him that we followed up by talking with Emily, and she denies anything happened. Let's see what he makes of that."

I said okay just as Kristy knocked on the door and Mike Singer came into the office. Showtime.

I directed Singer to his assigned place across from Karen. Following her script, I introduced her and told him we'd be recording the session. Then I told him about our conversation with Emily.

He sat bolt upright. "You're kidding. She denied that anything happened?"

"That's right," I said. "She says her text to Carol was just a joke. And she was annoyed that we're looking into it, although she's at least agreed to talk with us when she's back on Monday. What do you make of that?"

"I think she's afraid to bring accusations against her boss. Upton could ruin her career, and she'd rather sweep things under the rug than take that chance." He looked over at Karen. "You've dealt with these cases. What do you think?"

"That's certainly a possibility," she said, "but we're interested in why you think that. It could also be that nothing really happened."

"I doubt that. I was worried that something happened even before Carol showed me the text. There was something about the way Upton acted that made me suspicious. He was insistent that I wait in the car while he took her up to her apartment by himself, and then he seemed somehow relieved and in a good mood when he came back down."

"So that made you think that something had happened? Were you going to pursue it?"

"I was anxious to talk to Emily the next day, but she didn't show up for our scheduled meeting, and Carol showed me the text instead. It didn't sound phony to me. Plus, Upton's always been too friendly with his students, if you know what I mean. All hugs and having them over to his house and shit. I'm surprised none of them have complained. I guess this is the first time things went as far as they did with Emily." He shrugged. "Or maybe not. I suppose we don't really know."

"Tell us more," I said. "What's the gossip about Upton being too friendly with his students, and who have you heard it from?"

"Just what I said. He's too forward and touchy-feely with the women in his lab. It's all over the department. Carol didn't even want to work on a collaborative project with him at first."

"Okay, we'll ask her about that. We're going to be talking to her later." I looked over to Karen.

She picked up the cue. "I'd just like to go over a few of the things you told Brad and get some details pinned down, so we're clear on the record," she said. "You mentioned that all four of you went to the restaurant in your car, and you got there around six, right?"

Singer nodded.

"And when did you leave?"

"About eight fifteen. The time's on my credit card receipt." He pulled a credit card receipt out of his wallet and passed it over to her.

"Excellent. Now, you told Brad that you had a couple of pitchers of margaritas, and Emily got pretty tipsy." She looked at the receipt. "Three pitchers, as a matter of fact, according to this. Do you remember when she started feeling the liquor?"

"It was odd. It seemed to hit her all of a sudden at the end of the meal. She'd been fine, enjoying herself like the rest of us, and then something seemed to knock her for a loop. As if she'd been drugged."

"Are you suggesting that Upton put something in her drink? Did you see anything like that happen?"

"I think that's what happened. But no, obviously I didn't see him do it, or I'd have stopped him."

"Okay," Karen said. "So after dinner, you got everyone back in your car." She consulted her notes. "Dropped Carol off at her apartment and then went to Emily's. What kind of shape was Emily in then?"

"Out of it. She and Upton were in the back seat. She couldn't even sit up straight and was leaning into him."

"Did he touch her inappropriately?"

"I don't know. I was driving." Singer shrugged again. "Maybe."

"And when did you get to her apartment?"

"I'm not sure, probably a quarter to nine or so. I parked across the street, and Upton took her upstairs."

"Her apartment's on the second floor, right? Could you see anything from where you were parked?"

"A bit. I saw him get her in the door, and pretty soon the lights went on upstairs. The shades were open, and I could see them inside. Then the lights went off again, and Upton came back."

"Could you see what they were doing?"

"A little. I could just see their heads and shoulders. It looked like he helped her lie down on something, maybe a couch. After that, they were outside my line of sight."

"How long was he upstairs with her?"

"I'm not sure exactly. Ten minutes or so."

"Did he say anything when he got back in the car?"

"Something to the effect that the girl sure couldn't hold her liquor. And that he'd gotten her onto her couch and left her there, dead to the world."

Karen nodded. "And then you drove him back to the parking lot to get his car. What did you do then?"

"I went up to my office and finished up some stuff I hadn't gotten to during the day. Then I went home."

"How long were you in your office?"

"About an hour and a half. Why?"

"I just want to get a full picture for the record. Did anyone see you there?"

Singer raised his eyebrows. "You're asking if I have an alibi for later that evening? I'm the one who reported this!"

I stepped in. Maybe moderating these interviews was something I could do to help. "Don't be concerned, Mike. Like she said, we just need to get everything straight for the record. If Upton says he didn't do it, the only other possibility is that someone got into the apartment and assaulted her later that night. So we want to pin everything down as much as possible."

"Okay, fine. Yes, I stopped in the lab when I got there. Two of my students, Fred McElroy and Jane Watkins, were at their desks. Fred always works late, and I teased him about being a night owl. I stuck my head in again when I was leaving, and he was still there, working away."

"That would have been what, about ten thirty, when you were leaving?" Karen asked. "What were you doing in your office? Do you usually work late like that?"

"No, I usually leave by six or six thirty. But sometimes things just take longer. I had a bunch of emails stacked up that I wanted to deal with that night, so I took the opportunity to clear my inbox. Plus, I didn't really want to go home right away."

"I can appreciate the hard work," I said. "We all put in nights at the office."

Karen nodded. "Okay, I get it. But why do you say you didn't want to go home after dinner?"

Singer looked just a bit sheepish. "My wife is part of a neighborhood poker group, and it was her night to host the game. I really don't like it, and if I'd gone home at nine, I'd have been stuck in the middle of it. As it was, I got home a little after eleven—I live in Lexington, so it's about a half-hour drive. By then, people were leaving, so all I had to do was exchange some greetings. Then I went up to bed."

Karen smiled at him. "I can understand wanting to miss the poker game. Do you mind giving me the names of the people who were at your house?"

Singer shook his head. "You really are thorough. Sure, if you have some paper, I'll write them down."

I gave him a piece of paper and watched as he wrote some names on it. Then he handed it to Karen. "Is there anything else?"

"No, this is fine," Karen said. "I'm sorry if I seemed too aggressive, but I appreciate your cooperation. Do you have any questions for us?"

"There is one thing. The work Carol and Emily have done is really quite important." He looked over at me. "Did you hear her seminar today?"

"I did, and I agree. It has the potential of being a truly major advance."

"Which is why I hope it can be protected from the disgrace that's going to fall on Upton. There's no doubt that he needs to be punished, but it would be a tragedy if his misbehavior obscured the importance of our findings."

"I've already been thinking about that," I said. "Rest assured, I'll make it a priority to keep the science separate from Upton's behavior."

Singer turned to Karen. "These things usually end up in a negotiated settlement, don't they? With the guilty faculty member agreeing to resign and everyone signing a nondisclosure agreement? Could that agreement be set up to protect the science? I don't want to see Emily and Carol's discovery tainted by this kind of scandal."

"You're right," she said. "Negotiated settlements are common in cases like this. Which I hate because all too often, the guilty party winds up at another university and does the same thing all over again. But I agree that we have to protect the work of our students. I'll keep it in mind as things proceed and we talk with the dean about a resolution."

Singer got up. "Thank you, and don't hesitate to let me know if there's anything further I can do. That bastard can't be allowed to get away with this."

When the door closed behind him, Karen said, "He's an interesting character. But I don't think there was anything unexpected or inconsistent with what he told you earlier, right?"

"No. The only new thing he said is that there may be a history of Upton harassing students."

"Right. That'll be worth our following up on. Starting with Carol. When's she coming in?"

"Three thirty." I checked my watch. "About forty-five minutes from now."

"Good, I need a break. Is there anywhere nearby that I could get a quick bite to eat?" Her eyes twinkled. "You're right, I do need more than scones in my diet."

"Sure, there's a Starbucks in the Interdisciplinary Research Building, the shiny new glass building a block down to the right."

"Perfect. I'll be back in time for Carol." She got up and headed for the door. Then she stopped and turned around with a smile. "Unless you'd like to come have coffee or something with me?"

I looked at the stack of correspondence Kristy had piled on my desk, including two complicated-looking spreadsheets with little red stickers demanding urgent attention. But what the hell, there was something intriguing about Karen Richmond. The paperwork could wait.

I returned her smile. "Sure, why not?"

I felt a little twinge of anticipation as we left the office.

5

Starbucks was almost empty, so we got our food quickly and settled into a table in the back corner. A grilled chicken and bacon sandwich with some kind of a large, iced drink for Karen. Medium black coffee for me. I watched with amusement as she dug into her sandwich like a hungry teenager.

"Looks like you needed that. Are your days often so hectic that you don't have time to eat?"

She held up a hand and finished chewing. "Sorry, I don't mean to be a pig. But yes, sometimes things can get pretty crazy. And right now, I'm starved."

She took a gulp of her drink. "One good thing is that Singer has a solid alibi."

"Did you really think he's a suspect? Even though he's the one who told me about it?"

"Probably not, but we need to consider the possibility, even if it's only to rule him out. After all, he's the only one besides Upton who makes sense. He knew Emily was knocked out, and all he had to do was to go back to her apartment later."

I pondered that for a minute while she went back to attacking her sandwich. "Okay, but then how solid is his alibi, really? His students can presumably confirm that he went back to the lab and then left an hour and a half later. But during that critical ninety minutes, all we know is that he says he was in his office. Why couldn't he have gone back to Emily's apartment during that time?"

She looked up from her sandwich with a grin. "Ah, but he said he sent out a bunch of emails, right? That'll be easy for me to confirm on the university's server. They'll have the times they were sent and the IP address to verify that they came from his office computer."

I smiled and inclined my head in appreciation. "Of course, I didn't think of that. Pretty quick of you to jump on it."

She shrugged and went back to her lunch. "I've been doing this for a while. Computer records are often a big help."

"If you don't mind my asking, how'd you get into this? You don't seem like someone who belongs at a university. You're more like a trained detective."

"I am a trained detective. But how I got here is a long story."

It felt like she wanted to say more, so I gave her the invitation. "We still have twenty minutes before we need to go back. And knowing your background might help me work better with you."

She hesitated for a minute, then said, "Okay, you asked for it. A quick life story. I graduated from college in 2001 and was headed for law school. Then came the 9/11 attacks, and I felt like I had to do something to fight back. My dad was a cop, so I took the obvious course and joined the police department. I was good at the job, especially when it came to figuring things out, and I made detective after six years on the force. I sort of became a specialist in sex abuse cases and made my reputation by solving a big serial rape case that had everyone else stumped.

So there I was, moving full speed ahead and loving the job." She paused and looked me straight in the eyes. "Then my lieutenant decided that my way forward was in his bed."

My jaw dropped. "You're kidding!"

"Afraid not. I tried to deal with it tactfully, but he wouldn't take no for an answer. Eventually, I filed a complaint." She took a sip of her drink. "Bad move. That was 2008, and accusing a superior officer of sexual harassment wasn't something that cops did. The rest of the unit ganged up on me, and my husband took the opportunity to show his loyalty to the department."

"What do you mean? Didn't he try to help you?"

"He was a cop too. And the only person he tried to help was himself. He filed for divorce and testified in support of the lieutenant's claim that *I* had come on to *him*."

I started to reach across the table to squeeze her hand, but I stopped myself. I was beginning to like this woman, but I wasn't sure the gesture would be appreciated. "Shit, Karen, that's terrible. What a bastard."

She noticed and touched my arm fleetingly. "It wasn't much of a marriage anyway. He was more interested in teenage girls than in me. But it finished things off for me in the department, and I resigned."

I shook my head. "How awful."

"It wasn't the best period of my life—a double whammy of divorce and losing my job." She looked down at the table. "Eventually I pulled myself together and started thinking about what I could do next. The idea of joining a university police force appealed to me, and I applied for a couple of jobs. Almost gave up when I got turned down by men who checked with my former lieutenant for a reference, but the chief here was a woman. She listened to my side of the story and gave me a chance, so here I am. And it's a good place for me. Sexual harassment is a big problem in higher education, where there are so many situations in which one person has power over another. Faculty over their students, tenured faculty over nontenured faculty, graduate teaching assistants over undergraduates. I've had my hands full, but I think I've helped some young women avoid what I went through."

"That's quite a story, Karen. Impressive."

She snorted. "Oh, c'mon, Parker, cut the crap. And speaking of work, we need to get back and interview Carol." She got up and headed for the door. Then she turned to me with a smile. "Thanks for listening. Next time, it's your turn."

I followed her out of the coffee shop. Next time sounded good.

———

Carol was waiting for us when we got back, so I led her to my conference table and made the introductions.

This time Karen took the lead. "I think we should start by telling you that we talked to Emily this morning. She says nothing happened that night and that her text to you was just, well, she called it a spoof. What do you make of that?"

Carol fidgeted with her hands. "I know. She told me the same thing. But I don't believe it."

"What do you mean?" Karen asked. "You heard from her again after you got the text you showed Professor Singer?"

"Yes. She called me after you guys talked to her today. She was really angry that I showed her text to anybody. And this time she said it wasn't true. She was just playing with me. And I'd acted like a jerk and caused a lot of trouble."

"Why don't you believe her?" I asked. "Maybe this is all a false alarm."

Carol shook her head emphatically. "No, I really don't think so. Her first text was so hysterical and upset that I just don't think it was some kind of sick joke. It wouldn't be at all like Emily to make something like that up, and she doesn't play dumb tricks."

"So why do you think she's denying it now?" Karen asked.

"I think she got scared that she could get her advisor in trouble and wants to back off. He could destroy her career, and I'm sure she's frightened of what he'll do to her if she talks."

Her explanation echoed Singer's. I wondered if he'd discussed it with her after we interviewed him.

Apparently, Karen had the same thought. Maybe I was starting to get the hang of this investigator thing. "That's certainly possible," she said. "By the way, did you have a chance to talk about this with Professor Singer?"

"Yes," Carol said. "He stopped by the lab to see me after he finished his meeting with you. He thought the same thing as I just said."

"Well, it's true that victims in cases like this frequently balk at bringing charges forward," Karen said. "But it also seems possible that her first text really was a bad joke. Maybe she made it sound hysterical on purpose to fool you. Is there any other reason you think it's real?"

"I guess just all the rumors about Professor Upton and the way he acts with his students. Emily told me there were times when he got into her space and made her uncomfortable. Asking personal questions, touching her, giving her hugs. Lots of other students have said the same kind of things. It's common gossip in the department."

I nodded and made a note. Then Karen asked her to take us through the events of Tuesday night. Carol's account of the dinner was no different from Singer's, including Emily almost passing out in the restaurant and riding home with Upton in the back seat.

"One other thing I'm curious about," Karen said when she finished. "Why did you show Professor Singer the text from Emily instead of bringing it to Professor Parker or to the college administrative office that deals with these things? You thought Emily had been assaulted, so why didn't you report it through the normal channels?"

"I wasn't going to tell *anyone* because Emily's my friend, and she asked me not to. It only came out with Professor Singer because he was so concerned that she didn't show up for our usual meeting."

"What do you mean?"

"Emily and I meet with him every Wednesday to talk about the project. When Emily didn't come, he asked me if she was okay after Tuesday night. I tried to blow it off and just told him that she was probably a little hungover, but he kept asking if I'd heard from her. I said I hadn't, but I guess I looked uncomfortable, and he could see that I was lying. He became very stern and insisted that I had to tell him the truth. He was worried about her. Then I sort of broke down and showed him the text."

———

After Carol left, Karen looked at me with a faint smile. "So what do you make of all that?" she asked.

"I don't know what to think at this point. It could be that Emily's pretending nothing happened because she doesn't want to go up against Upton. But it's also hard to discount the possibility that her first text really was nothing but a bad joke."

"We'll need to get an answer to that out of Emily. But I'd also like to find out more about the department gossip on Upton. Can we arrange to talk with some of the students?"

Her phone started ringing before I could answer. She looked at it and said, "Hang on. I have to take this."

She stiffened in her chair as she listened. "I'll be right there," she said and hung up.

She closed her eyes and shook her head. "There's been a new report of a faculty member assaulting a student. It sounds ugly, and I have to get over there and talk to her. Christ, that makes two already this month."

"How awful. Should I line up some students and Upton for tomorrow?"

"No. I suspect I'm going to be tied up with this tomorrow. Why don't you go ahead and interview the students yourself? You know what to ask, and they might be more open talking to you alone anyway. Tomorrow's Friday, so if you get that done, we'll be ready to talk to Emily on Monday. Let me know when your admin has a time set for us to meet with her. In the meantime, I'll check out Singer's alibi. I want to hold off alerting Upton until we do that and hear what Emily has to say."

I watched her leave the office. Another case of sexual assault by a faculty member. It seemed like an epidemic. I suspected that I'd learn more from Karen at some point.

I asked Kristy about the meeting with Emily on Monday. She'd already sent Emily an email and was just waiting for a response from her confirming the time. Then I grabbed my coat and headed back over to the research building. It was late in the afternoon, but the students would still be around. And probably more comfortable if I talked to them on their home ground than they would be in my office.

6

One of the perks I got for being department chair was that the dean provided funds for a senior research associate to help run my lab. The idea was that having someone experienced enough to help guide the students and keep things on track would make up for the time department administration took away from my research. I'd been lucky enough to find an associate who was smart and well trained but didn't want to be an independent faculty member with her own lab—especially not with the responsibility of competing for the grants that would be necessary to support her students. Having Janet as a sort of general lab supervisor helped a lot, although it still was a far cry from having my own time free for research.

Perhaps the most important thing Janet did was to keep in close touch with the students. She was a good mentor, close to their own age and always available to talk, so they tended to confide in her. Which made picking her brain a good way for me to get a feel of the department gossip.

When I reached the research building, I took the stairs up to my lab on the fourth floor. Whatever little bit of exercise I could add to my daily routine seemed worthwhile. I shared the floor with three other faculty members, so I walked down to my lab and went in the first door off the main corridor. The look and smell of science always gave me a good feeling. This was where I belonged. Not in my department chair's office. And most certainly not stuck in meetings at the dean's headquarters.

There were six lab benches that jutted out perpendicular to the windowed back wall, some late afternoon sunlight still streaming in. Each lab bench had a desk associated with it, right next to the window, and the benches themselves were covered with equipment and paraphernalia for doing research. Microscopes, tabletop centrifuges, pH meters, automatic pipettes, test tubes, bottles of chemicals, and so forth. On the opposite wall, there were some large pieces of equipment—refrigerators, freezers, biohazard hoods, and incubators for growing cells. Janet and my three graduate students were all there. It was a much smaller group than it had been before I became chair, when I had nine students, two research associates, and a technician in the lab. But I'd reduced the size of my group in recognition of how much of my time was spent on administration. Three students were about all I could keep track of these days, even with Janet's help.

Janet was at her desk immediately opposite the door I entered, focused on her computer. "How're things going?" I asked.

She looked up with a start, then smiled. "Not bad. How's the world of university administration?"

"Hectic, as usual. I'm over here partly to see some real science for a change but also because I need to ask you something. Has to be kept confidential, okay?"

"Of course, you know that's not a problem. But before you get into that, be sure to check in with Laurie while you're here. She has some seriously good stuff. You'll love it."

Janet was a scientist herself—she knew what really got me going. I inclined my head with a smile. "Thanks, I will. But first, I want to get your take on student gossip. Do you hear anything about Steve Upton and how he interacts with his students?"

She shrugged. "Sure, there's gossip about all the professors. A lot of students like Steve, say that he's very warm and supportive, always available to talk with them, and usually has helpful suggestions when they have problems. But there are also some stories about women in his lab who've felt uncomfortable when he's gotten too close. Hugging them when they've gotten good results, rubbing their shoulders, asking personal questions, that sort of thing. But most of his students say that's just how he is and that he pretty much treats the guys in his lab the same way. He seems like one of those professors who may be too buddy-buddy with his students, but I don't think there's anything really wrong."

Interesting; not quite the picture Carol had painted. But maybe a tendency to step over the line. I headed toward the far end of the lab, where I saw Laurie at her desk.

"Hi, Laurie. Janet tells me you have some interesting news."

She looked up at me with her freckled face split by a big grin. "I do! The experiment I set up with Josh Cohen gave a neat result. Look here."

She opened her notebook, and I pulled up a chair next to her to look at the data. "You remember we're looking for a drug that makes cancer cells more sensitive to radiation, right?"

I rolled my eyes. "You think I've lost all my intelligence just because I'm a department chair? I can still manage to remember what you're working on."

She laughed. "Well, check this out. Treating cancer cells with this drug, AX824, makes them three times more sensitive to a standard dose of X-rays. And most important, it doesn't have any effect on normal cells. Meaning it could really enhance cancer treatment by radiation."

I scanned through her results. Approximately 20 percent of either normal or cancer cells died after receiving a standard X-ray dose. But if the cells were pretreated with AX824, cancer cell death increased to 60 percent, whereas normal cell death stayed about the same at 20 percent. Pretty interesting results.

I gave her a fist bump. "You're right—this looks really good. You should be able to develop this into an important paper and a nice thesis."

She jumped up and put her arms around me. I got up and started to return the hug, but then I wondered if I was being too forward. What would my other students think? Was this the kind of thing Steve Upton did?

I patted her shoulder instead and sat back down. "I want to ask you about something else. Josh is in Steve Upton's lab, isn't he?"

"Yes. You remember he synthesized this drug and asked me if I could test it in our cell culture system. You said it was fine to collaborate with them."

"Sure, it's great. A nice collaboration between chemistry and biology labs. But tell me, how does Josh like working with Steve?"

"Josh likes him a lot—although it's funny. He says that Steve is sometimes so friendly it's embarrassing. Like one time, Josh got some nice data, and Steve gave him a big hug in front of the whole lab." She giggled. "I guess like I just did to you. Anyway, Josh said that if he'd been a girl, he would've thought Steve was trying to feel him up."

I sent Karen an email when I got back to my office.

Talked to two of my students, including one who's collaborating with a student in Upton's lab. It seems like Upton may be overly friendly and demonstrative, hugging and so forth. But no indication of real harassment. I think we should hold off questioning more students until we talk to Emily on Monday, just to be sure we don't start spreading new rumors.

How are you doing with your new case? Give me a call tomorrow or over the weekend if you want to discuss.

I almost suggested meeting for a cup of coffee or a drink but decided that was probably too pushy. I kept checking my email but didn't get a response for the next three days, which I used to catch up on other stuff in the office. Going into work on weekends gave me a chance to bring Rosie in with me, which she always seemed to enjoy. As did my students, who loved having a dog around to play with.

Finally, a terse message came in from Karen on Sunday afternoon.

Thanks for the info. Been busy. See you Monday morning for interview with Emily.

I read it over twice, looking for some indication of the warmth I had felt from her Thursday afternoon. But there wasn't any.

Maybe I'd misinterpreted her friendliness over lunch.

7

Karen got to my office just in time for our eleven o'clock meeting with Emily, who was already waiting in the visitors' area. I offered coffee, which they both declined, and we took our usual positions at my conference table. Emily was wearing standard student garb, jeans and a T-shirt, with her long black hair pulled back in a ponytail. Given the occasion, I was surprised at how relaxed she seemed. Comfortable and at ease, with no sign of nervousness.

I started off by introducing Karen and said, "Emily, I just want to say again that we're here to help you. We have to explore further what may or may not have happened Tuesday night, but I want you to know that we're on your side."

She smiled pleasantly. "Thank you, Professor. But like I said on the phone, nothing happened. Except that I drank too much and woke up with a stupid hangover."

Karen pushed a piece of paper across the table and addressed Emily. Her tone was harsh. "Is this the text you sent to your friend Carol? Read it. It doesn't sound like nothing to me."

Emily turned red. "I'm sorry. I was just kidding, like I said."

Karen gave her a hard look and leaned across the table. "Kidding? Emily, I find that hard to believe. Let me explain something to you. Like Professor Parker said, we want to help you. But at the same time, your text suggests that there's been a serious violation of university policy governing sexual harassment. We're obligated by federal law to pursue the case, and we have no intention of doing otherwise. We need your full cooperation, and anything less will mean that you're obstructing our investigation. If I find that to be the case, I can and will recommend your dismissal from the university."

That had the effect Karen wanted. Emily's lower lip quivered, and her eyes filled with tears. "All right, I'm sorry. Please, I have to finish my degree. I'll cooperate."

Karen sat back and nodded to me, passing the baton. "Okay, let's start over," I said. "Tell us what happened Tuesday night."

She sniffled and asked for a glass of water. I got a bottle for her from my undercounter refrigerator, and she started talking. "Our professors, Mike Singer and Steve Upton, took Carol and me out for dinner at a Mexican restaurant to celebrate our paper. We were having a good time, eating and drinking, and I guess I had too much to drink. When we were finished with dinner, I started to feel really tipsy and couldn't even walk out of the restaurant without Carol helping me. We all got into a car, but after that, I don't remember much. I think I was in the back with Steve, and I sort of remember him helping me into my apartment. And that's it. When I woke up the next morning, I was on the couch with my pants and underwear pulled down."

She started crying again, and I passed her a box of tissues. "I don't remember what happened or how I got that way. And I don't want to get Steve into any kind of trouble. I can't imagine that he did anything, and he's always been so good to me."

Karen changed her tone, speaking softly and sympathetically now. "Thank you for telling us. It's possible that you'll remember more later. One thing I'd like to suggest is that you get some help dealing with this. It's not healthy for you to just try to bury it." She handed Emily a business card. "Dr. Stamford in Student Health is an expert at helping women who've been assaulted. I know her well, and she's a good person. Is it okay if I refer you to her?"

Emily nodded, and Karen reached across the table to squeeze her hand. "Good, I'm so glad. You're going to be all right, Emily. You're strong, and you'll get through this."

Emily gave a faint smile. I was amazed at the transition Karen had made, from a tough interrogator to a compassionate support figure in minutes. I guessed it was another indication of her training as a detective. She was good.

"Can I ask you a couple more questions?" Karen said.

Emily nodded again, and Karen continued. "You think Steve Upton helped you up to your apartment from the car, right? Can you remember how you got into the apartment? Did you give him a key?"

Emily was quiet for a minute. Then she frowned and said, "I do sort of remember that. I fumbled around for the key in my jeans pocket and gave it to him."

"And do you remember where it was the next morning? Was it back in your jeans?"

"No. It wasn't in my pocket, and I didn't know where it was at first. Then I found it on my kitchen table. He probably left it there instead of giving it back to me."

"Was your door locked the next morning? Did it look normal?" Karen asked.

"Yes, it was locked. Like always."

"What kind of lock do you have?"

Emily looked confused. "I don't know what it's called. Just a regular doorknob that a key goes into."

Karen picked up her phone from the table. "Hang on a sec." Then she showed the phone to Emily. "Is your lock like this?"

"Yes, just like that."

"We'll talk more about it later, but this isn't a very secure kind of lock," Karen said. "It's easy to open with just a credit card if you know how. I'm going to get it changed to a deadbolt for you. The university will cover the expense."

Emily blinked her eyes and took a nervous sip of water. "I didn't know. Thank you."

"But first, tell me—are there any other keys?"

"The owner who lives downstairs has a key. And I keep a spare hidden underneath a big potted plant by the door to my side entrance."

"And does anyone else have a key? A boyfriend maybe?"

"I broke up with my boyfriend a month or so ago. He had his own key, but he gave it back to me. Although I think he knows about my spare."

The logic of letting the ex-boyfriend know about the hidden key escaped me, but Karen didn't react. "We'll need your ex-boyfriend's name," she said. "How was the breakup? Was he angry?"

"Derek Kilpatrick. He's a student here too. And yes, he was furious about the breakup. He has a terrible temper, and I'd had enough of his tantrums, so I told him we were finished. He had a fit and kept bothering me for the first couple of weeks. Finally, I told him I was going to call the police, and he stopped."

"What do you mean by bothering you?"

"Catching me unexpectedly on campus or even coming to my apartment to beg me to take him back. And then yelling and cursing at me when I wouldn't."

Karen made a few more notes and looked over at me. "Anything you want to ask at this point?"

I turned to Emily. "Yes, I'd like to hear about your relationship with Steve Upton. What's working with him been like?"

"It's been great. I'm lucky to have him for my thesis advisor. He's always available to help, and he's totally supportive, not like the advisors some of my friends have who seem to just be out for themselves."

"Has he ever asked you to do things socially with him, other than your dinner Tuesday night?"

"I've been over to his house a couple of times for lab parties with other students. And one time he got tickets to a Red Sox game and took four or five us with him. But he's never asked me to do anything alone with him. He's friendly but always very professional. That's why I can't believe he did anything to me Tuesday night."

"There seems to be a lot of gossip about him being overly physical with his students. Hugging, rubbing backs—that kind of thing."

Emily rolled her eyes and looked annoyed. "That's silly. Yes, he's an expressive guy, and he'll get excited and be demonstrative if you get a good result. Or try to be comforting if you're upset. He's hugged me a couple of times, but it doesn't mean anything. And he's the same with the guys in the lab. It's just the way he is. Nothing wrong with it."

I nodded and looked over at Karen. "Okay, thanks. That's it for me."

Karen reviewed her notes. "You said the key was on the kitchen table and the door was locked. Was everything else like it normally is the next morning? Lights, windows, anything out of order?"

Emily closed her eyes, as if she were trying to picture the scene. "I'm pretty sure the lights were off, like usual. And the windows were closed with the shades most of the way up, the way I always keep them."

Karen made a note and closed her book. "Good. That covers all of my questions for now too. Can I send a couple of technicians over to your apartment to see if there's any physical evidence from Tuesday? You know, fingerprints or DNA."

"Okay, I guess. Where would they look?"

"How about the clothes you were wearing that night—have they been washed?"

"No. They're still in the dirty laundry."

"Good. We'll take a look at them. And the couch you slept on? Was there a cover over it?"

"No. It's just an upholstered couch."

"They'll check that out too, then, as well as look around the rest of the apartment to see if they can find anything. Also, I'll send a locksmith over to change your lock. And please don't give out any extra keys, okay? Or make duplicates to hide. It's just too dangerous."

Emily blushed. "Okay, I won't. Do you think someone could have used one of my keys to get in Tuesday night?"

"I don't know," Karen said. "There seem to be at least a couple of possibilities, obviously including Professor Upton. We're just going to have to keep investigating."

Emily got up to leave. "It wasn't Steve. I can tell you that for sure. He's always been a perfect gentleman."

———

Once we were alone, I looked across the table at Karen. "My head's spinning. What do you make of all that?"

She smiled wryly. "At least she's talking to us now. And we know her text wasn't a sick joke. But you're right—it doesn't make it clear what happened."

"It seems like a couple of people had keys or knew about the hidden spare. Including the ex-boyfriend, who sounds like a real jerk. Plus, he could easily have had a copy of his key made before he gave it back to her."

Karen nodded. "He certainly sounds like a plausible suspect. And we don't know about the landlord. Not to mention that anyone could have gotten through her lock without much trouble anyway. The only thing that seems clear is that Emily does *not* think it was Upton."

"So are you ruling him out?"

"No. He's still the most straightforward suspect. But we also need to consider the alternative that someone else went to her apartment after Upton left, found her knocked out, and took advantage of the situation to assault her. Maybe the crime-scene techs will come up with something to help us. I wouldn't be surprised if they find semen or hair on the couch, although getting a match could be another story."

I nodded. "But it wasn't just random, right? Whoever it was presumably knew that Emily was passed out before they came in and assaulted her, didn't they?"

"Yes, I think that's a reasonable assumption. Which means that the assailant is likely to have seen Upton taking her up to her apartment. Maybe the ex-boyfriend was in the neighborhood, still stalking her. Or maybe the landlord heard or saw something."

"How about Singer? Are you still considering him as a potential suspect?"

"No, his alibi checks out. Students saw him coming and going from his office, and his wife's poker friends verified that he got home around eleven. And there were a bunch of emails sent from his office computer during the time he was there."

"Okay," I said. "That still leaves us with some other possibilities to sort out. What's next?"

She smiled with a warmth that excited me. "Next, we go get some lunch. Then I think we're ready to talk to Steve Upton. But let's see if we can surprise him in his office instead of bringing him over here."

"All right. I'll have Kristy check if he's in today. But why the change in venue?"

Again the smile. I liked it.

"Just feel like an outing," she said. "It'll make lunch more of an adventure."

8

It was one of those late-fall days when Boston weather was un-expectedly pleasant. Sunny and midseventies. Karen suggested that we get lunch from the Italian sausage truck and take it down to the river, so we got sausage, pepper, and onion subs and found a bench on the edge of the Charles. Joggers kept passing by on the path behind us, but otherwise, we were alone with the river and a couple of ducks.

I saluted her with my can of soda. "A Monday picnic. This is an unexpected treat."

"Just a working lunch to give us a chance to talk. How're you doing with all this? I'm sorry I didn't get back to you over the weekend. I was just totally bombed with the other case I mentioned."

I smiled inwardly as I took a bite of my sub. It was nice that she mentioned her failure to respond to my email. "No problem. Don't worry about it. How's that going?"

"It's a mess. It seems that the victim's thesis advisor has been harassing her for years, threatening that she'd never get her PhD if she didn't have sex with him. She went along, didn't feel she had any other choice, but finally, she decided to stand up to him and filed a report. Now the problem is that he denies it all. Says that she's always been a weak student, and he's talked to her about leaving the PhD program, so she's just making these charges as revenge. Leaving us with a classic case of he said, she said. There have been previous allegations against the professor, so I believe the student. But I'm not sure if I'll be able to get to the bottom of it and actually prove anything."

I shook my head in disgust. "Terrible. It's just so sad how common that kind of behavior is. And most men still manage to get away with it."

She sighed. "Yes, all too common. And what happened to Emily is the next step in the progression. A date-rape drug followed by assault, and often the victim can't remember anything after being drugged. Unless we have a bit of luck, cases like this never get solved."

I tossed the ducks a piece of my sub roll. "You still think that's what happened to Emily? Upton slipped something in her drink at the restaurant?"

She shrugged. "That's the simplest explanation. Although jilted ex-boyfriends are also good suspects in cases like this."

"Like that Derek jerk?"

She finished her sandwich. "Yeah, like him. But Steve Upton's the one who had the opportunity to drug her, so he's still our best bet. Let's go chat with him."

———

Upton's office was empty when we got there, but the door was open. He was apparently in the building, so we went across the hall to his lab. It had the same basic design as mine, but it was twice the size and had one wall taken up with four large chemical hoods, which were needed to accommodate the part of Upton's research that involved the synthesis of new drugs. Each hood was a floor-to-ceiling, vented cabinet, with a glass sash window in front to protect the operator from toxic fumes in the work area. Two of the hoods contained glove boxes, which completely separated the researcher from whatever nasty stuff went on inside them.

I spotted Upton talking to a young man—presumably one of his students—at a desk near one of the hoods in the back of the lab. We went over, and Upton got up and waved when he saw us. He was casually dressed in jeans, sneakers, and a well-worn green turtleneck that was fraying at the cuffs. His thick, horn-rimmed glasses and long black hair, in need of a trim, completed his look as a harried academic who didn't have time to worry about his appearance.

I introduced Karen as a member of the dean's office. Upton, in turn, introduced the student as Josh Cohen. "You might not know it," Upton said, "but Josh is working with one of your students, Laurie. They have some nice data with one the compounds he's synthesized."

I shook Josh's hand. "I do know about it. Laurie showed me her data last week. Looks promising."

"So is that what you wanted to chat about?" Upton asked.

"No, there's something else," I said. "Can we go to your office?"

His office was standard faculty issue in the research building. About a hundred and fifty square feet with a U-shaped desk in the back, under the window. A colorful poster from a conference on the Greek island of Mykonos hung on one wall and a big whiteboard, covered with chemical formulas and equations, on the other. The front of the room held a small, round conference table, big enough for meeting with two or three students.

We sat at the conference table, and I said, "We're here to talk about your student Emily and what happened to her last week."

"Oh, don't worry about that. I know she missed the weekly seminar, but her mother had a fall, and she needed to go out to Chicago and help. She emailed me Wednesday morning, and she's back today. She's a good kid. It's too bad she wasn't at Carol's talk, but it couldn't be helped."

I started to say there was more to it than that, but Karen spoke up before I could get the words out. "You say she emailed you Wednesday morning? Could we see that, please."

Upton looked surprised but said, "Sure, I'll print it out."

He did so and handed copies to both Karen and me.

Hi Steve-

Sorry about this, but my mom had a bad fall and is in the hospital. She's all alone, so I came here to be with her. Just landed in Chicago. I'll keep you posted but should be back in the lab next week.

And thanks for helping me home last night. Guess I had too much to drink at dinner!

Emily

Karen and I looked at each other. It had been sent at eleven thirty, some three hours after the text to Carol. Emily had gotten herself back together quickly. And it didn't seem like the kind of email she'd send to someone she suspected of having assaulted her.

"I'm afraid it's more complicated than this email suggests," Karen said. "She sent another text a few hours earlier to Carol Hopkins, one of Mike Singer's students."

"Of course. I know Carol. She's Emily's collaborator."

She handed him a copy. He turned pale as he read it.

"My God, she's saying she was attacked that night! This is horrible. Have you talked to her? What happened?"

"We've talked to her, but she apparently passed out and doesn't remember anything. We're hoping you can help us figure it out."

"I wish I could, but I don't know anything."

I stepped in so that Karen didn't have to do all the work. "You and Mike Singer took Carol and Emily out to dinner that night, right?"

"Yes, to celebrate their paper. Like Emily says, she had too much to drink and was barely able to walk when we finished dinner. Mike drove us to her apartment, and I got her inside. She basically passed out on her couch, and I left."

"Have you been out drinking with her before?" I asked. "Or taken her out for other social occasions?"

He frowned. "What are you implying? I know the rules. I don't date my students. This was a celebration dinner with another faculty member. I've had Emily over to my house a few times for parties with my other students, but never alone."

"Okay," I said. "Just had to ask."

He glared at me, and I gave Karen a nod, signaling that she should take over.

"How did Emily hold her liquor on those occasions?" she asked. "Did she ever have a problem like Tuesday night?"

"No, never. She'd always have a few drinks and enjoy herself, but she never got drunk or lost control. Tuesday was weird—maybe a combination of excitement about the paper and one too many."

Karen nodded. "What happened after dinner, then? Did you help her out of the restaurant?"

"No. Carol walked her out of the restaurant, and we all got into Mike's car. He dropped Carol off and then took us to Emily's apartment. Then I got her out of the car and up to her apartment, like I said."

"How'd you get into her apartment? Was it locked?"

"Yes. Emily gave me the key."

"What did you do with it when you left?"

"I put it on the kitchen table, so she'd find it in the morning."

Karen stopped to make a note, and I asked, "Did you lock the apartment when you left?"

"Of course I locked it. Do you think I'm an idiot?"

Upton didn't seem too fond of me this afternoon. I went back to letting Karen do the talking.

"How long were you up there?" she asked.

He shrugged. "Just a few minutes."

"Can you tell us exactly how you got her onto the couch?"

"What do you mean?"

Karen leaned forward and spoke with an edge to her voice. "Were you holding her close to you? Maybe touching her breasts? Or seeing down her clothes? We can understand how something exciting could have happened."

Upton turned red and sat up straight in his chair. "Are you crazy? You're accusing *me* of assaulting her? That's ridiculous."

He looked as if he were going to attack Karen, so I held out a hand. "Calm down, Steve. We just have to ask, okay? You can see how this could look. You took her up to her apartment, and then she passed out and woke up naked."

"Do I need a lawyer? I'm not sure I want to say anything else to you people."

"A lawyer is up to you, but we have to find out as much as we can about that night," Karen said.

Upton took a deep breath and sat back. "I don't know what to say."

"You can start by answering the question," I said. "Did you get too close and fondle her when you put her on the couch? Yes or no?"

"No, damn it, I didn't touch her in any way that was inappropriate! I was holding her with my arm around her shoulders and eased her onto the couch; then I swung her legs up. I'm not interested in unconscious women. Ask Singer. The lights were on, and he could see from the street."

"The shades were open?" Karen asked.

"Yes. I could see Singer in his car."

"Did you close them when you left?"

"No, I don't think I bothered. I just turned off the lights."

"Okay," Karen said. "Did you see anyone else on the street, either when you were outside or in Emily's apartment?"

"I don't know. I wasn't paying attention. I don't remember anyone."

"All right, then what?"

"Nothing. Mike drove me back to my car, and I went home."

"You live in Cambridge, right? What time did you get home?"

"Probably around nine thirty. I have a condo near Harvard Square."

"Was anyone with you?"

Upton gripped the table and leaned forward. "What difference does that make? Screw this!"

"Look, we need to get everything pinned down for that night," I said. "So again, just answer her question."

"I live alone. You know that. I watched TV for a bit and went to bed." He seemed to get control of himself. "Now what are you suggesting? You think I went back to her apartment and assaulted her later?"

"If you didn't do it when you took her upstairs, someone had to have gotten in and assaulted her later. It would have been easy enough for you to leave the door unlocked or keep the key and go back when Mike Singer wasn't watching from the street. So we need to know where you were."

He clenched his jaw. "Well, I told you. I was home."

Suddenly the rage seemed to evaporate, and he just looked sad. "For Christ's sake, I'd never hurt her. I didn't do this. Just get whoever did."

———

We were quiet until we left the building and were alone. Then Karen asked, "What do you think?"

I shook my head. "Why do you always ask me that first? What do *you* think?"

"Detective training. I'm always after information, not interested in giving it out. So you first."

"Well, his story matches everything else we know. Except if Singer was watching from the street, it would have been hard for him to have done anything when he took her upstairs."

"Yes, I want to take a look at the scene and see what kind of view Singer would have had," Karen said.

"So you still think it was Upton?"

"He's certainly the obvious candidate. If it wasn't him, we have to believe someone else came back later and found her. Whereas Upton could have planned it from the beginning, drugged her, and been right there in the apartment to do what he wanted with her."

"I don't know. I can see where he looks like a strong suspect. But my gut is that he's not the one. Emily obviously doesn't think it was him, and something about his manner makes me believe him."

She frowned. "Well, my money says it's him. But I do agree that we need to check out any other possibilities."

"And how do we do that?"

She looked at her watch instead of answering. "I have to get back to the office for a meeting now, but do you want to join in with me tomorrow and find out?"

"Wouldn't miss it," I said.

She smiled. "Meet me at Emily's apartment at ten."

9

I started the morning in my chair's office and got a brief update from Kristy on the missing twenty thousand. Still missing, although she thought there was new hope. Carlson, the college financial guy, had apparently decided that she wasn't an idiot and was actually trying to help her trace the money.

I made some encouraging noises and promised I'd spend more time with her on this later. But my mind was elsewhere. Not just on the case but on Karen. Something about the sharp and sexy detective fascinated me. I was glad when it came time to leave the office and walk over to Emily's apartment. Maybe today's outing would be followed by another lunch together.

Emily's address turned out to be a two-story, yellow colonial on a tree-lined street in Brookline. Karen was already there, parked across the street in a red Subaru. I waved to her and was happy to see her hop out of the car, a welcoming smile on her face.

"Thanks for coming," she said, giving my arm a little squeeze in greeting. "It's a lot more fun doing this with you than on my own."

I felt like giving her a hug, but this wasn't the place. So I just smiled. "Thanks, I like working with you too."

She gave me a wink that was just a shade flirtatious. Or at least I hoped so.

"Good," she said. "Then let's start by checking out the view of the apartment from here. I want to see what was visible to Singer. You go upstairs, turn on the lights, and stand by the window. Then go around to the couch and bend over like you were putting Emily down on it. Or messing with her while she was lying down. I'll see how well I can follow you." She handed me a key.

"Does Emily know we're doing this?" I asked.

"Yes. I told her we were coming over this morning. She's already at the lab and said it's okay to make a quick visit. The crime-scene techs were already here, so you don't need to worry about touching anything."

"Did they find anything interesting?"

"Too early to tell. No semen stains or anything obviously indicative of sexual assault. They took her clothes and got samples for DNA analysis from the couch, the door, and the windows. They were there yesterday, and I put a rush on it, so we should get the results soon, and we'll see if there's anything that doesn't match Emily or Upton. He cooperated and gave the techs a sample for comparison, so we'll be able to tell if anyone else was there."

Karen got back in the car so that she'd have the same view that Singer had had. I crossed the street and went to the side door leading up to Emily's apartment. The door was now fitted with a deadbolt as well as the ordinary lock, both of which opened with the same key. When I was upstairs, I went over to the window behind the couch. Karen was clearly visible across the street, and she waved to me. Then I walked around to the front of the couch. Karen was still there, and we waved again. She moved her hand in a downward motion, and I bent down as if I were helping someone onto the couch. At that point, my view of her was lost. I straightened up slowly and found that I could see her again when I was bent about 45 degrees at the waist, no more. She gave me a thumbs-up sign and motioned me back. We'd seen what we needed to.

She was waiting for me outside the apartment when I got back downstairs. "That was useful," she said. "Singer could have seen him get Emily to the couch, but he would have lost sight of them if Upton bent over or kneeled down. So Upton could have assaulted her without being seen, even with the window shades open."

"I guess. I just can't get around how Emily insists it wasn't him."

"I understand, but I wouldn't take what Emily says too seriously. She can't remember, and she may just be protecting him. Either because she genuinely likes him or because she's afraid of bringing accusations against her boss. Anyway, let's see if we can dig up anyone else who may have seen something. Starting with the landlord."

We walked around to the front of the house, past a large pine tree in the front yard and a garden area filled with pansies and brightly colored chrysanthemums. A small, wiry, gray-haired woman, probably in her seventies, answered the bell. Karen showed her detective's ID and introduced me as her partner.

"I'm Jane Harkness," the woman said. "Is there something I can do for you?"

"Your tenant Emily had a problem upstairs last Tuesday night," Karen said. "Can we ask you a few questions about that evening?"

"What happened? Is she all right?"

"I'm sorry; we're not at liberty to give out any information about it. But yes, Emily's fine."

Mrs. Harkness frowned. "Well, if you can't tell me what happened, I'm not sure how I can help."

"Just a few questions, please," Karen said. "Were you and your husband home that evening?"

"My husband passed six years ago; it's just me now. And yes, I was home."

"I'm sorry for your loss," Karen said. "Did you see Emily that evening? We believe she got home between eight thirty and nine."

"I did see her then. A car pulled up across the street, and a man helped her out and around to her side entrance. It seemed like he was supporting her, and I thought she must have really gotten drunk. I was surprised. That's not like her."

"Could you tell if he went up to her apartment with her?"

"I think so. I could hear heavy footsteps upstairs for a few minutes. Then it was quiet, and the man came back down and got in the car."

"Thank you. That's very helpful. Did you notice anyone else on the street? Either then or later in the evening?"

"I was curious about the car bringing Emily home, so I kept looking out the window until it went away. There was another man in the car who waited for the one who took Emily upstairs, and that was it. Nobody else. I went to bed soon after, but you might want to ask AJ. She lives a few houses down and has a dog that she always walks later at night. Maybe she saw someone. Her house is the blue one across the street."

We thanked Mrs. Harkness for her help and promised to keep her informed as far as possible. Once we were back in the garden area, Karen said, "Okay, that eliminates the landlord. Let's go talk to the neighbor."

We walked across to the blue house and rang the bell, to be greeted by loud, frantic barking. Karen held up her badge, and a woman opened the door, holding the source of the barking in her arms. The woman was fiftyish, with blonde hair and piercing blue eyes. The dog was thirty or forty pounds, white with orange markings. It was squirming and howling as if it wanted to eat the invaders.

Karen said, "Oh, a PBGV! I love these guys," and reached out to pet it. The dog immediately stopped barking and nuzzled against Karen's hand. The owner smiled and said, "Yes, that's Beantown. Or Beanie, for short. He likes you."

I followed Karen's lead and ventured to pet Beantown, to be similarly rewarded by happy licks. Especially when he smelled Rosie. "What's a PBGV?" I asked. "He's lovely, but I never heard of them before."

"It's short for Petit Basset Griffon Vendéen," the owner said. "He's a French hound, a hunting dog. I have a friend who breeds them."

"A hunting dog? Seems like he's more of a lover," I said. Beantown acknowledged the compliment by reaching up to give me a wet lick on the nose. We were all friends now.

"You should meet his mother, Cleo. Hunts rats, squirrels, opossums. She's the terror of the neighborhood. I'm AJ, by the way."

Karen introduced us and asked AJ about last Tuesday evening. She'd been sitting near the window and had seen a car pull up and a man help Emily to her apartment. The poor girl must have had too much to drink. The lights in the apartment came on for a few minutes. Then they went off again, and the man came back down and drove off in the car.

"Did you see anyone else on the street?" Karen asked.

"Not then, but I did see a strange man when I took Beantown out for a walk a little later."

"What time was that?"

"Maybe half an hour or so after the car left, maybe a bit longer. He was walking up the street in the opposite direction from us. He seemed in a bit of a rush."

"Can you describe what he looked like?"

"Big." She looked at me. "At least two or three inches taller than you and bulky. Not fat but hefty, like a football player or something. He was wearing a hooded jacket, and I couldn't see much of his face, although I could tell he was white and had a beard."

Karen nodded. "Good, that's very helpful. Anything else about him?"

"Just that Beantown didn't like him. He pulled away when we saw him and didn't want to get near him. And Beanie loves everybody."

———

"So what did we learn from all that?" I asked while we walked back to Karen's car.

"Well, quite a bit about PBGVs. And what do you think about the big guy on the street?"

"He does sound like an odd character. We should try to track him down, but how do we even start to do that?"

"Hang on," she said. "I'm a trained detective." She pulled out her phone and scrolled through it. Then she handed it to me. "How about this?"

I looked at the photo of a young man with a beard. He was standing next to a car, which gave me a size comparison. Big and bulky, but well put together. Like AJ had described.

"Where'd this come from?" I asked.

"I looked up Derek Kilpatrick, Emily's stalker ex-boyfriend. Who may very well either have a key or know where the spare was hidden, remember?"

I pursed my lips and nodded. "All of which makes him a good suspect. Especially if he was in the neighborhood that night."

"Yup, at least he's a viable alternative. He's on the wrestling team and lives in the Delta Tau frat house. His first class is an hour from now, so we could probably catch him at the fraternity now. Want to pay him a visit? I'd like you with me for this one. He looks like kind of a macho customer."

"I'm supposed to be meeting with Kristy to continue some financial stuff we started earlier, but I can put that off. Are you afraid he might attack you or something?"

She gave me a mocking laugh. "No, I can take care of myself in that department, thank you. I just think he may be the type that'll have more respect and give better answers if a man's asking the questions."

10

Delta Tau was located on Beacon Street, just a few blocks from my place. Parking on the street was impossible, as always in downtown Boston, so Karen double-parked in front of the frat house and put a police placard on the dashboard. She was blocking off one of the two lanes of traffic, but that was also common Boston practice.

I knocked on the door. No answer. I kept knocking, and it was eventually cracked open by a sleepy-eyed hulk wearing nothing but sweatpants.

"What do you want?" Part question, part growl.

Karen held up her badge and said, "We need to talk to Derek Kilpatrick."

Hulk stared at the badge as if he was having difficulty comprehending. Finally, he opened the door, pointed to the right with his head, and said, "Kitchen." At least his head was good for something.

I almost tripped over the assortment of bicycles and dirty dishes that covered most of the living room floor. The distinctive smell of marijuana was overwhelming, which was probably good, considering what else the place might have smelled like.

Maybe the pot explained his hesitation in letting us in. Karen had the same thought because she said, "Don't worry—we don't care about the marijuana."

"Legal in Massachusetts anyway," Hulk muttered. "Screw yourselves."

We found the kitchen and spotted another bulky young man sitting at the counter with a mug of coffee. This version was also dressed in sweatpants, but he wore a T-shirt and had a book open in front of him. He had a beard, and Karen asked if he was Derek Kilpatrick.

"That's me," he said. "Can I help you?"

She showed him the badge. "We'd like to talk to you about Emily Jackson."

He snorted. "I haven't seen her in weeks. She broke up with me." He turned his back on us and concentrated on his coffee.

Since Karen had suggested he might be more susceptible to a male touch, I took over. I used the voice I reserved for intimidating students, which was sometimes a necessary part of being a college professor. "But you still keep an eye on her, don't you? And know where she keeps her spare key."

"Who gives a shit? Everyone knows where that bitch keeps a spare."

He hadn't bothered to look up from his coffee, so I decided to go still more forceful. "So where were you last Tuesday night when she was assaulted? Did you use the key to get into her apartment while she was asleep?"

"Go screw yourself! Whaddaya think I am?"

"For all I know, you're someone who assaults women in their sleep."

The transition to movement was surprisingly quick for a guy with so much bulk. He jumped up and swung at me with a roundhouse right. It would have hurt if he'd connected, but I managed to duck and let it go harmlessly over my shoulder. Then I hooked my left leg behind him and shoved hard on his chest. A maneuver I'd learned on the playground in the fourth grade, when I was the target of a bully who didn't like my new glasses. It still worked. Derek Kilpatrick went down hard on his ass, just like Johnny Frank had nearly forty years ago.

He looked at me in shock for a minute before he spoke. "You son of a bitch, how the hell'd you do that?"

I shrugged. "Pretty easy when the only punch you throw is a big, sloppy roundhouse."

He groaned and looked at the floor. "Shit."

"So are you ready to answer our questions now? Where were you last Tuesday night?"

He glared at me, and I wondered if he was going to jump up and try another shot. But then he relaxed, and I could see the fight go out of him. "I was at the library studying for a chemistry exam the next day. Can't exactly study around here. And unlike some of these guys, I'm a good student. Premed."

At least premed fit someone Emily might have dated. But he needed to work on his bedside manner. I started to tell him so, but Karen stepped in before I had the chance.

"What time did you get there?" she asked. "And when did you leave?"

"I had dinner here with the guys first, so I probably got there around seven or seven thirty. I think it was around eleven when I left and came back here."

"Did anyone see you there? Maybe someone you chatted with."

"Shit, lady. I went there to study, not to socialize. I guess the students at the front desk saw me."

Maybe it was an alibi of sorts, but I wasn't convinced. I looked over at Karen. She shrugged. Nothing more to get from him. We left him on the floor, probably still trying to figure out how he'd gotten there.

"You handled him pretty well," Karen said when we got back to the car. "Had some training?"

"New York public schools. Bullies were the same then as now. Glad I was there to take care of him for you."

She snorted. "Thanks, but dealing with a big jerk like that isn't a problem. I would've ducked his punch like you did. And then kicked him in the balls instead of knocking him on his ass."

I inclined my head in a gesture of acceptance. "You said you could take care of yourself. What'd you think of his story?"

"Let's see if any of it checks out." She started thumbing through her phone, ignoring the angry drivers honking and trying to get around us. "Okay, he is taking a chemistry course." She paused as she continued scrolling. "And yes, its syllabus does list an exam scheduled for that Wednesday."

"So that part's real," I said. "But it doesn't mean he was at the library Tuesday night."

"No, of course not. I'll see if we can pin anything down by talking to the students who were at the front desk that night. But we'll have to keep him on our list for now."

Her phone beeped to announce an incoming text. "Hang on a minute—let me look at this. I just got a message from the lab."

Maybe this would be the break we needed. I mentally crossed my fingers.

Karen smiled grimly when she looked up from the phone. "Well, I think this helps. There was plenty of Upton's DNA all over the place, including on Emily's clothes. But nothing from any third party. So we don't have any suggestion from the forensic evidence that anyone else, like our friend Derek, was at the scene. Looks like Upton's our guy."

"Wait a minute," I said. "We knew Upton's DNA would be there. I don't see how that finding adds anything."

She raised an eyebrow. "Yes, but the point is that we didn't find any trace of anyone else. No mythical other assailant."

"Sure, but they could have cleaned up after themselves. Or worn gloves."

"C'mon, Professor, use some of your brain power. They couldn't have gotten rid of their own DNA but still have left Upton's, right? And as for gloves, you'd have to assume they went in with gloves on, planning on the assault. The only way that makes sense would be if someone saw Upton hauling Emily up to her apartment, so they knew she was vulnerable. But we have two witnesses to her being dropped off, and neither of them saw anyone else on the street."

"What do you mean? AJ saw somebody who looked just like Derek."

"But that was later, remember? Not when Emily was taken up to the apartment."

"Okay, fine. I see where you're coming from. But I don't think we can eliminate Derek. Maybe he just came by later, let himself in, and found her vulnerable on the couch."

"And how would he have known to wear gloves? That's asking for a lot of coincidence. Look, I'll check out Derek's alibi further. But all the evidence says that Upton's the straightforward pick for this. He was in the restaurant to drug her, took her upstairs, and did his thing. And his DNA's all over the place. Why are you having problems with it?"

"Because Emily swears it wasn't him, and the stories about his coming on to students don't seem to hold up. And my gut tells me it wasn't him either. Plus, I don't think we can eliminate Derek. He's a premed student. He could have had gloves with him from a lab or something."

"Emily might very well be protecting her advisor so that she doesn't lose momentum in her thesis work. And you're asking for an awful lot of coincidence with Derek. Even if he had gloves, how would he have known to use them?" She paused and looked at me with a frown. "I'm sorry, but I don't think you're looking at this objectively. What's your relationship with Upton anyway?"

"What do you mean? I'm on good terms with him, like I am with most of my faculty."

"It's a little more than that, isn't it? Didn't Upton say when we met him that one of your students is collaborating with one of his—Josh, the guy he introduced to us? How's that going? Sounded like they had some good results."

I returned her stare. "Maybe they do. So what? What are you implying?"

She continued to glare at me. "What do you think? I'm worried that you don't like him as a suspect because it would endanger your research."

Now I was angry. "That's ridiculous!"

"Is it? Perhaps, but I can't afford to work with someone who has a conflict of interest in a case. Or even the appearance of a conflict."

"What's that supposed to mean?"

"It means that I need to back off and get some distance from you."

It felt like a slap in the face. "Karen, c'mon, that's ridiculous."

She turned away and started the car. "I also need to get back to my office for a meeting. You'll hear from either me or the dean at some point about our next steps."

I got out and watched her drive away. Great. Instead of a nice lunch, Karen was pissed at me about Steve Upton.

I went a block out of my way and walked back to my office along the river, trying to enjoy watching the people walking their dogs. It didn't work. I was too preoccupied.

Why couldn't I accept Upton as the guilty party? It seemed clear enough to Karen. But I had the same feeling in my gut that I sometimes got about a research project in the lab.

Something just didn't seem right about the obvious answer.

11

Kristy gave me a big smile when I got back to my office. I was grateful. It was nice to feel like someone was happy to see me. Her desk was covered with notebooks and spreadsheets, which I guessed must be a source of good news.

"You look busy but happy," I said. "Still hunting for the missing twenty thousand?"

"Yep. And I think we're getting there. Ed's been a big help."

"Ed?"

"Ed Carlson. You know, the college financial guy."

I raised an eyebrow. "The same Carlson who acted like such a jerk at our meeting with the dean?"

"You wouldn't know it, but yes, the same guy. I traced the deficit to a shortfall in our travel reimbursement from research accounting, but I couldn't figure out what went wrong. So I went to him and admitted defeat. At first, he acted like I was a moron and went back through all my numbers himself. But when he hit the same blank wall as I had, he started to get interested."

"Hold on, you mean it's not some kind of simple mistake in the books?"

"Not on my end anyway. And once Ed was convinced of that, he dug in and wanted to help figure it out." She smiled. "We're buds now."

I wished I could say the same about Karen and me, but I wasn't so sure at the moment.

"Congratulations, I guess accounting makes strange friends." Although given Kristy's sexual orientation, not bedfellows. Which was where I had to admit that I hoped Karen and I were heading.

I mentally slapped myself to refocus. "So what's going on?"

"It's a discrepancy in our travel budget and reimbursements from central research accounting. Basically, I gave out more money in travel funds to our faculty than I got back from central."

"I'm not sure I follow. How could that happen?" I had to admit that I didn't know how the process of travel reimbursements worked. It was one of those bureaucratic details I avoided worrying about. That's what administrators like Kristy were for.

She looked at me with a faint smile. "You don't even know how the process works, do you?"

"Actually, no. It's one of those things I'm happy to leave to you."

"Okay, here's a crash course. You know that our faculty members travel to attend all sorts of conferences and meetings. Their trips usually wind up being covered by grant funds, but it can often take several months before those expenses get paid. So I give out advances from department funds first and then send people's receipts on to the research accounting office for approval and processing. Then the department gets paid back from research accounting when the money eventually comes in from whoever is paying for the trip."

"Seems simple enough. What's the problem?"

"Last year I apparently gave out twenty thousand more than I got back from central. Nineteen thousand, four hundred and fifty-two, to be exact."

"Can't you just check the travel advances you gave out versus central accounting's records?"

"That's the way it should work. And why Ed thought I was an idiot when I couldn't reconcile it. But their records match mine, except the actual money we received falls short."

"I don't get it. You mean there were bills that went to central, and they didn't actually pay the money back to us?"

"That's what it looks like. But I can't figure out what requests those were, and research accounting won't tell me. At first, they insisted the problem was in my records. Then Ed pushed them, and someone higher up finally said that some of our reimbursements were being delayed because of a random audit, but he wasn't at liberty to provide any details. That got Ed really mad, so he had Dean Houghton send them a memo, and he thinks that'll get them to tell us what's going on. And hopefully give us our money."

I rolled my eyes. "What a nuisance. Mysterious random audits, like the IRS or something. Oh well, at least you've got the dean's office on our side now."

I proceeded into my office. No wonder I couldn't keep my mind on science. As if Steve Upton wasn't enough, now it looked like the department budget was entangled in some kind of bureaucratic bookkeeping mess.

And then there was Karen. Had I blown it with her?

I checked my email. At least there were no new crises. But there *was* an interesting one from my student Laurie.

I've got some more nice data with a new compound from Josh. Even better than before! Are you going to be around so I can show you? I'd like to plan out what we should do next with this.

I smiled to myself. Good for her. And a chance to escape from fretting about Karen and think about science for a bit. I responded that I'd be right over and headed back out the door.

———

Laurie was working at one of the cell culture hoods when I got to the lab. The hood was a six-foot-long cabinet with a glass sash separating Laurie from the cultures she manipulated inside it. She was wearing purple latex gloves and a lab coat to protect the sterile cell cultures from the bacteria and yeast on her skin.

"Here I am," I said.

She looked up with a smile. "Great. Thanks so much for coming over. Just give me a minute, and I'll show you the good news."

She continued adding fresh culture medium to a dozen dishes on a metal tray in the hood. When she finished, she stood up and transferred the tray to a nearby incubator. Then she removed another tray containing six dishes. "We can look at these. They're from my newest experiment and really make the point."

I followed her over to a microscope on the lab bench in the rear of the room. We both sat down, and she put a dish under the scope. "Start with these," she said. "Untreated normal cells."

The dish was filled with healthy cells, triangle-shaped, with nice, round nuclei in their centers. "Okay, these look nice," I said.

"Now look at these. Normal cells after a low dose of X-rays."

She put a new dish under the microscope, and I scanned it. Most of the cells were healthy, but some were now dark and shriveled up. Dead cells.

"All right. Maybe ten percent dead."

"And now these are normal cells treated with Josh's drug and then x-rayed."

I looked again. "About the same as X-rays alone."

She smiled. "Right. Now for the good part. Start with these—untreated cancer cells."

Nice healthy cells, although different from the normal ones. I could tell they were cancerous because they were rounder and had odd-shaped nuclei. I gave the dish back to her, and she gave me a new one. "Now cancer cells after X-irradiation."

"Like the normal cells, about ten percent dead," I said.

She gave me the last dish. "And now the winner. Cancer cells after irradiation *and* Josh's new drug."

I looked again and did a double take. This culture was almost completely filled with dead cells. "Wow, this is at least eighty percent killing! Amazing. Even better than what you showed me before."

She grinned ear to ear. "I knew you'd like it. This new compound Josh made really works!"

"It sure does," I said. "An increase like this in killing cancer cells without an effect on normal cells could be a big deal in radiation treatment. You're right. We should plan out what to put together for a paper on this."

"Hang on a minute." She bent down and pulled a paper bag out of the bottom drawer of the lab bench. "Here, this is for you to celebrate."

"What is it?"

"Look and see."

I opened the bag and pulled out a bottle of my favorite single malt. I laughed. "Why thank you. But how'd you know what to get? This is the scotch that I always drink."

"Don't you remember the Christmas skit? The whole department knows your favorite scotch."

I rolled my eyes. "Ah yes, I remember."

It had been a holiday skit where the students had done mock news reporter interviews with three or four faculty members, including me. They'd asked what I did when I got home after a hard day. I told them I had a glass of scotch. Then they asked what I did after a good day, and I said a glass of scotch. And so forth. I didn't remember telling them my favorite brand, but I guess I had. So it seemed that my drinking habits were public record in the department. How nice.

"Well, that's kind of embarrassing," I said. "But thank you. I'll enjoy this tonight. What will you do to celebrate?"

"Oh, don't worry. I'll make sure Seth takes me out for a nice dinner." She gave a little wink. "But seriously, do you think we should talk with Josh and Professor Upton? I'd like to plan out the rest of the experiments. One of the questions is whether we should test more compounds. Josh says he could synthesize other derivatives to see if we can get one that works even better. Or should we publish what we have first and then make more derivatives for a second paper?"

I considered for a minute. I wasn't sure I wanted to get more involved with Upton, given his status as the prime suspect. And Karen's concerns. But Laurie was right. We needed to talk with them to decide how to proceed. And I wasn't going to let Karen's unfair accusation that my judgment was compromised interfere with Laurie's progress. I was perfectly capable of keeping the science separate from the assault case.

"Yes, we should meet with them," I agreed. "Can you set something up?"

She smiled. "I thought you'd say that. Josh and Professor Upton are both upstairs now, expecting that we may come up. I'll send Josh a text that we're on our way."

Laurie grabbed her notebook, and we took the stairs up to the eighth floor. Upton was in his office, sitting at his conference table with a lanky young man that I recognized as Josh. While Laurie and I took the remaining two seats at the table, Josh turned on a PowerPoint projector that was hooked up to his laptop. Then he went over to Upton's whiteboard and began to review the relevant features of the drugs he'd synthesized.

The first drug that Laurie had gotten results with had a double-ring structure with twelve carbons. Josh explained that he'd modified this by adding chlorines to several different positions. Laurie had so far tested three of these and one, with a chlorine added to carbon number 10, was the compound that had given the remarkable results she showed me today. Testing of the others was in progress, and Josh suggested that he could make derivatives with several other chemical groups added instead of chlorine. Maybe the new compound could be made even better.

Laurie also wanted to test the compounds on several different types of cancer cells to determine the generality of their action. In addition, she thought it would be a good idea to see whether Josh's drugs made cancer cells more sensitive to anticancer drugs, like they did to irradiation. If so, they could play an important role in chemotherapy as well as radiation treatment.

Upton and I exchanged glances and nods of approval. These kids were good. The two of them had obviously thought this through, as if they were seasoned investigators. We had little to add except encouragement and congratulations on a job well done. This was one of the biggest rewards that came from being a thesis advisor for a graduate student—watching students become independent enough to develop their own research plans. I basked in Laurie's progress, and judging from Upton's encouragement, he was feeling the same about Josh.

When Laurie and Josh excused themselves to go down to the lab and work out some experimental details that didn't need our input, I asked Upton how Emily was doing.

"Surprisingly well," he said. "She seems like her normal self, working hard in the lab and interacting with me and the rest of the group just like always. She's been to someone in student health that your detective colleague recommended, and she says that seems really helpful. How about on your end? Are you making any progress in figuring out what happened?"

I wasn't about to touch that one. Certainly not to fill Upton in on our progress. "Working on it, but not there yet."

I'd been struck by Upton's focus on the science and obvious pride in Josh earlier. And he certainly seemed straightforward and supportive in talking about Emily. If he was Emily's assailant and worried about our investigation, it was an impressive act. Or he was innocent and not thinking about it. My mind was still open on his involvement, but this meeting made it still harder for me to picture him as a pervert.

I started to leave the office, but he got up and walked me to the elevator. When it stopped on our floor, he offered his hand and said, "Thanks for what looks like a good collaboration." We were shaking hands when the elevator door opened, and Mike Singer stood there, looking at us.

I got into the elevator and exchanged brief greetings with Singer before he returned to talking to the woman beside him. When he did, I politely faced the front of the car and let them continue their conversation without interruption. But I could feel his eyes boring into my back as the elevator descended.

12

I went back to my office and spent the afternoon dealing with relatively normal things—faculty requests for departmental research support, graduate student funding, teaching schedules, and the like. The standard department administration wasn't the kind of fun working with Laurie on her experiments had been, but it was better than dealing with sexual assault. Especially because Karen's focus on Steve Upton gave me an uneasy feeling about the way the case was going. But she was the pro, and I needed to step back and let her do her job. And for my own sanity, I needed to get over the idea that something more was developing between us. Whatever sparks seemed to sometimes fly, our differences in viewing the case created a conflict that clearly made it impossible to develop the kind of personal relationship I kept hoping for.

That litany all made sense until Karen's email came in toward the end of the day.

Brad, I'm so sorry about this morning. I had no reason to be short with you, and I apologize. I know you're just trying to help. And I realize that you know Upton much better than I do, so I need to pay attention to your instincts.

Can I make it up to you over dinner tonight? Carmella's in the North End at seven, my treat.

I read it twice, with a growing feeling of excitement and anticipation. Surely this meant that Karen was interested in more than talking about the case. Meaning there was hope for our budding relationship after all. The rest of the afternoon passed slowly.

———

The North End, aka Little Italy, was one of my favorite parts of Boston. Less than a mile square, it had a distinctly European feeling, with its maze of narrow streets lined by Italian bakeries, groceries, and restaurants. The population was about one-third Italian American, down from virtually 100 percent in the 1930s, but you could still hear Italian spoken on the streets.

I took a rideshare to avoid the parking hassle and had it drop me off at the downtown end of Hanover Street. It was a pleasant evening, and I strolled up Hanover, past two of my favorite bakeries and the Paul Revere House. When I got to Charter Street, I turned left toward Carmella's, which was also in the direction of the Old North Church and Copp's Hill Burying Ground. The Puritan ministers Cotton and Increase Mather, famous for their roles in the Salem witch trials, were buried there. An omen that I hoped was not a reflection on the way the current investigation was going.

Carmella's was the kind of small, intimate restaurant the North End was known for, with murals of old Italy hanging on exposed brick walls and vases of dried flowers on the tables. Karen was already seated at a corner table with an open bottle of wine. I joined her, and she poured me a glass.

"It's a Chianti Classico. I hope you like red."

I took a sip. "Nice. And this place looks good. Haven't been here before."

"It's one of my favorites. I think you'll like it." She smiled. "Even better than your neighborhood Starbucks."

"I certainly hope so." I put my menu aside. "If it's one of your favorites, what do you recommend?"

"Well, the eggplant rollatini is a fantastic appetizer, but it's a lot. Want to share?"

"Sure, that sounds good."

"And then you'll have to choose your own entrée. I've never had anything bad here, so you're on safe ground."

The waiter greeted Karen by name when he came to take our orders. I went with veal marsala, Karen with the chicken parmigiana.

I took another sip of wine. "Looks like you're a regular here."

"Yes, I live just a couple of blocks away, so I'm probably in once or twice a week. Sometimes for takeout and sometimes to eat here."

"Really, you live here in the North End?" This seemed like the chance to ask the obvious but overly personal question on my mind. "Alone?"

She looked at me with a faint smile. "I love the ambiance. Been here over ten years now. And yes, alone. How about you?"

"I have a condo in Back Bay, right on Commonwealth Avenue."

Her smile broadened. "And the other part of the question?"

I felt myself flush. "Yes, alone."

"How nice. I like the whole Back Bay neighborhood. Have you ever been married?"

"I gave it a try once, but it didn't mesh with the demands of doing science. My wife wasn't happy with all the nights and weekends I spent in the lab, especially after we had a kid. We stuck it out for several years, mostly for our son's sake, until we finally admitted that we were just making each other miserable."

"I'm sorry," Karen said. "It can be tough combining marriage with a demanding career. How do you get along with your son?"

"We're good. He's a lawyer in Los Angeles—got married himself a couple of years ago. My ex and I are actually on pretty good terms now too. Better than for most of the time we were together."

"And how about living alone? Do you like it, or do you get lonely?"

I shrugged. "I'm fine on my own. Maybe I'm too busy to be lonely." I smiled to lighten the mood. "Especially now that you have me moonlighting as a detective's assistant."

She reached across the table and squeezed my hand. "Happy to help."

Was there a hint of a different kind of help to come? I was trying to figure out how to respond when the waiter came with our appetizer. I let the thought go and tried the eggplant.

"Delicious," I said. "Good recommendation."

"Thanks. I'm glad you like it. I'm hoping a nice dinner will serve as an apology for my being a bitch this morning."

I swirled my wine. "Don't worry about it. You're the pro, and I can see where the forensics left you pretty well settled on Upton. And how you don't want my nagging doubts to hold you back."

"True enough, but it wasn't fair of me to accuse you of bias. I have a lot more respect for you than that. Anyway, I hope the rest of your day went better."

"As a matter of fact, it did. It turned out to be one of those rare days when we get a really promising result in the lab." I told her about Laurie's experiments as we ate our appetizer and the waiter brought our entrées, discreetly omitting Laurie's name so that she didn't recognize this was based on my collaboration with Upton. That had become an inconvenient truth, and I didn't want to retrigger her reaction of this morning. I'd deal with it later, if necessary.

She raised her glass in a toast when I finished. "Congratulations. That sounds great. But is it really so unusual to get good results like that?"

"Very unusual to get something like this, actually. People get results and publish papers all the time. But something really important, like this could be? You maybe get something like this a few times in your career, if you're lucky. Or sometimes not at all."

"Important results must not be so unusual for you, though. After all, you've got the top position in your department."

I laughed at that. "No, that's not how it works. Department chair isn't really the top position, and it's not particularly based on research accomplishment, although you need to have a solid record to get the respect of your colleagues. But being chair is more of an administrative task that you do for a limited period, usually five years. After that, you go back to being a regular faculty member."

"Doesn't sound as if you like it much. Why'd you agree to do it?"

A good question. I gave her my best shot at an answer. "Well, it was hard to say no with both my colleagues and the dean asking me to take it on. And it *is* giving me the chance to bring in some new young faculty and have a hand in shaping the future of the department, so that's a good thing. On the other hand, it's really taken me away from research, and I've been worrying about keeping my lab going. I guess that's partly why I'm so pleased with these new results."

She furrowed her brow. "Interesting. It's so different from my world. For me, promotion to the top is the only way to go. And it's a fight to get there, not something I'd ever be asked to take on as a chore."

There was a look of determination in her eyes. I asked, "Are you in the middle of a promotion fight now?"

She nodded. "That's actually the meeting I had to get back to the department for this morning. The chief is retiring and the search for a successor is in full swing. I'm pretty sure that I'm the top internal candidate, but they're also looking at an outsider."

"Do you know who?"

She hesitated and frowned. "Unfortunately, I do. It's the asshole who harassed me years ago on the Boston force."

"Oh shit, I'm sorry! Do you really think he could get it?"

"I hope not. I wouldn't have much of a future here if he does. But I think it's mine if I have the dean's support."

I finished my veal. "Great. I'll make sure I get a chance to put in a good word for you."

She smiled and clinked my glass. "Thanks, I'd appreciate that. What I need to do is to get this case closed. Everything's in now, and bringing it to a successful conclusion will be a big plus on my record. And in the dean's report on me."

I drained my wine as I thought about it. I wished I could make it easy for her, but I couldn't do it. "I just don't know. I agree with you about the evidence, but there's nothing solid against Upton either. And I'm not so sure we can dismiss that idiot wrestler."

"I did follow up a bit more on his alibi. One of the students who works at the library confirmed he was there that night. Although she couldn't be sure of the time."

"So his alibi's still shaky?"

She sighed. "Well, it's certainly not airtight. But what he told us holds up, and he really wasn't positioned to be the perp. He had no way of knowing Emily was knocked out and vulnerable. The only one besides Upton who did know that is Mike Singer. And his alibi's about as solid as it can be."

"I know—I have to agree that Upton's the obvious choice. I guess I just can't get around the fact that Emily insists it wasn't him."

"At least you admit that everything points to Upton. I guess that's some progress. And you're right that it's not conclusive without something from Emily. Meaning there isn't any possibility of criminal charges. But I think I'm going to go to the dean with what we have and see how she wants to proceed. There may be enough for her to push Upton into a negotiated resignation. I hope you won't stand in my way?"

I frowned. "If she asks, I'll have to tell her I have reservations. But this is your case. I won't try to sabotage you."

The waiter brought the check and asked if we wanted coffee or dessert. Or, he suggested, maybe some grappa. Karen looked at me with a faint smile and a wink. "Why don't you come over to my place for an after-dinner drink instead?"

Wow! Unless I was misreading this, it was an invitation to take our evening far beyond dinner. "I'd love to. Just let me make sure that Rosie's taken care of."

She raised an eyebrow. "Who's Rosie? I thought you lived alone."

"I do, as far as other humans are concerned. Rosie's my pug, and I just need to text my downstairs neighbor to tell her I'm going to be late. She'll take Rosie down to her place for the night."

I sent Ellen a quick text and then pulled up the video feed from my condo. Rosie was sleeping in her bed in the living room, snoring away with her usual pug noises. I showed Karen the phone.

"See, here's Rosie. Happily napping, which is mostly what she does when I'm not there."

Karen looked at the phone and broke out laughing. The sound of Rosie's heavy snoring seemed to particularly amuse her. "You have a whole system set up to monitor your dog when you're away? You must be one of those totally crazy pet owners!"

I felt myself flush. She'd hit it right on the head. "I guess I have to plead guilty to that. I was worried about leaving her alone when I first got her, so I set this up so I could look in on her when I was out. Fortunately, Ellen, the girl who lives downstairs, is great about taking care of her when I'm away, so Rosie's just fine. But I still like to peek in on her occasionally."

Karen shook her head and finished her wine. "Nice to know you're a nutcase."

The waiter brought the check, and she signed it. No credit card. I looked at her quizzically, and she said, "I have an open account. It's the North End way. Walk me home?"

Her condo was three blocks away on Salem Street, in a midrise red-brick building that was typical of the North End. When we got there, I followed her up an ornate marble staircase to her unit on the second floor. The living room boasted gleaming hardwood floors, a white leather couch facing a granite fireplace, and peach-colored walls with two large oil paintings.

"This looks great," I said.

She murmured, "Glad you like it."

Then she moved into my arms and pressed her mouth against mine. The kiss deepened, and I held her to me, exploring the warm, smooth skin beneath the back of her knit blouse.

Then she moved away and took my hand. "Why don't I show you the rest of the house? The bedroom's just off to the right."

13

Sunlight was beginning to fill the room when I woke with Karen beside me. I snuggled closer to her, and she rolled over on top of me with a soft moan. This time was less frantic but maybe even better than the night before. We clung to each other afterward, transported for a while to a world where nothing else mattered.

Finally, she got up and made coffee. I followed her into the kitchen, and we sat holding hands at her breakfast table, smiling and gazing at each other like young lovers. Then she got up and kissed me. "I wish we could stay here all day, but I've got to go to work. How about I grab a quick shower and get ready? Then I'll drop you at your place so you can get some clean clothes. Are you free tonight, I hope?"

"Sounds good," I said. "Especially the part about tonight."

It was almost ten thirty before I got to my office. I couldn't get my mind off Karen. I didn't know where we were going, and our differences over Upton could still become a huge problem. Especially given how important this case was to her. But for now, I was well and truly smitten. I hadn't felt this way for a long time.

———

The call to a three o'clock meeting in the dean's office came in the early afternoon, less than two hours beforehand. Not her style to operate on such short notice, meaning that something was up. I was pretty sure what it was, and I wasn't surprised to find Karen sitting in the waiting area when I arrived. A distinguished-looking man with short white hair, dressed in a navy blue, pinstripe suit with a textured red tie and gold cufflinks, sat opposite her. I recognized him as Richard Fried, the university lawyer with whom the dean worked on occasions when legal advice was required. Fried and I had collaborated on a case a few years ago when a junior faculty member who had been denied tenure sued the university. I greeted him just as the dean's assistant appeared to usher us into the inner sanctum.

The dean was already sitting at her conference table, and I was surprised to see Mike Singer next to her. She introduced him to the lawyer as we took our seats and got down to business. "I appreciate all of you coming on such short notice. Karen informed me earlier today that the investigation of the assault on Emily Jackson has proceeded as far as possible, so I want us to review the case and consider our alternatives with the advice of counsel. I asked Mike to be here not only because he first reported the incident but also because he's expressed concerns to me about the outcome, particularly the need to distance the research he's done with Upton from the possibility of scandal. Karen, could you please start by summarizing your findings?"

Karen ran through the story as we knew it, concluding that the evidence against Upton would never be conclusive without an identification from Emily, but that everything pointed to him as the perpetrator.

The dean asked Singer if Karen's summary was consistent with his recollection of the night. He nodded and made a dismissive hand motion. "It's simple. He drugged her at dinner, took her upstairs, and fooled around with her. What's to question?"

The lawyer nodded. "It does seem pretty straightforward. As Karen says, it's not a prosecutable case without victim testimony. But our standards for action at the university level are substantially lower than the standards of criminal law. Our proceedings require only a preponderance of the evidence, not proof beyond a reasonable doubt, and I think there's a reasonable case here against Professor Upton. Of course, I'd recommend that we give him an opportunity to resign rather than face formal termination proceedings."

The dean looked at me. "Brad, you've been working alongside Karen on this. Anything to add?"

I wished I could just say no and let Karen have her day. The last thing I wanted was to mess this up for her, especially after last night. Not to mention the chief's job hanging in the balance. But I just couldn't do it. "I'm sorry, but I still have doubts about this. Karen and I have talked about it, and she's the pro, so I understand that it makes sense to defer to her judgment. But I'm just not convinced it was Upton. Emily insists it wasn't him, and we can't rule out the possibility that someone else, including her abusive ex-boyfriend, came in later that night. In the face of that, I don't feel comfortable concluding that he's the guilty party."

The dean frowned, and Karen looked away. I knew this hurt her. She started to say something, but Singer burst out first. "I don't suppose your doubts have anything to do with your collaboration with him! I saw the two of you cozying up to each other. You've got a project going with him that could save your whole damned lab. Of course you don't think he's guilty, you little shit! Talk about bias."

"Is that true?" The dean glared at me. "You have an active collaboration with Upton?"

I felt like I'd been punched in the stomach. All I could do was look down at the table and nod.

Then she turned to Karen. "And did you know about this? An obvious conflict of interest, but you didn't think it was a concern? Not even worth telling me about?"

Karen swallowed hard. "I just learned about it two days ago, when Brad and I interviewed Upton. Apparently, one of Brad's students is doing something with one of Upton's. But we talked about it, and I'm confident that it doesn't affect Brad's judgment."

Singer turned to me with a loud, snorting sound. "That's bullshit. I asked Upton's student Josh what it was all about after I saw you and Upton being all buddy-buddy yesterday afternoon. He said that you all just had a big collaborative meeting and that it's something really important. Saying that it doesn't affect your judgment is a load of crap."

Karen looked at him, openmouthed. "The meeting was yesterday afternoon?"

"Yes, yesterday," Singer said. "And you don't think it affects his judgment." He looked like he was about to spit on the floor in disgust. "How gullible can you be?"

"Shit," the dean said. She kept her focus on Karen, making no attempt to suppress her anger. "Even if it doesn't affect his judgment, just the appearance of a conflict like this could undermine the entire investigation. How the hell could you ignore this?"

Karen turned red and tightened her lips. Before she could answer, I jumped in and tried to deflect the dean's anger. "Look,

I just heard about this project with Upton last week from one of my students. It's something she started with a student of his, and it does not, repeat *not*, impinge on my analysis of this case."

The dean shook her head. "It's a little hard to accept that when you're the only one standing up for him. And even if it's true, it creates a messy situation." She moved her eyes back and forth between Karen and me. "I'm really disappointed in both of you."

Karen looked down at the table and spoke in a soft voice. "I'm sorry. I should have informed you immediately."

"Indeed," the dean said coldly. "Nonetheless, here we are." She turned to the lawyer. "Richard, what's your recommendation?"

"Despite Professor Parker's supposed reservations, I think the case against Upton is pretty clear. My recommendation is that we prepare an agreement asking for his resignation, in return for a terminal year of paid leave and the usual nondisclosure guarantees that'll allow him to find a job elsewhere. Then we confront him and give him a choice between accepting that or facing sexual misconduct proceedings, which would inevitably go public."

Singer interrupted. "It's also important that any such settlement includes his agreement to give up all rights to participation in the future development of Immunoboost. This is a major discovery, and I don't want to see it tainted by his name any longer. Particularly for the sake of the students who've done the work."

The lawyer gave the dean a questioning look, and she nodded agreement. "Fine," he said. "I'll include that in the agreement. Professor Singer, can we get together on this afterward so you can help me with the wording?"

Singer nodded, and the dean said, "Good. If the two of you can get that drafted, I'll have Upton called in tomorrow morning."

Just then Karen's phone rang. The dean gave her a sharp look of annoyance.

"I'm sorry," Karen said sheepishly. "This is my emergency number. I have to take it."

She got up and went to a corner of the room, speaking softly so that we couldn't hear her. When she came back to the table, she was looking more like her normal self. "Maybe you should hold off on meeting with Upton," she said. "That was Dr. Stamford in student health. Emily's starting to remember more of what happened that night. She wants to talk to us."

There was a moment of stunned silence. Then the dean said, "Okay, go see what she has to say. I'll wait to hear back from you before I set up the meeting with Upton." Turning to me, she added, "Brad, you stay out of this from now on. I think we've had enough of your opinions."

"I hate to say this," Karen said, "but Emily specifically asked that Brad and I talk to her together. I guess she feels more comfortable with him because she knows him. I'm afraid that Brad needs to be there when I interview her."

The dean threw her hands in the air. "Oh, for Christ's sake, can't we get out of this mess? All right, go ahead." She got up from the table and gave me a look that would shrivel stone. "Just try not to screw things up with any more half-assed conclusions. I want this done and Upton out of here."

———

Karen had nothing to say as we walked together to student health. Not the companionable silence of friends and lovers, but a wall of hostility between us. She ignored my attempts at conversation about Emily, so I tried an apology. "Look, I'm sorry things got messy in there. The last thing I wanted was to undercut you with the dean. But don't worry—she'll calm down, and I'll make it right."

She looked up at me with a pinched face and eyes that were bright and moist. "I can't believe you didn't tell me you had a big meeting with Upton yesterday. And that Singer saw you. How the hell could you set me up in front of the dean like that? Your whole collaboration with Upton has backfired, just like I was afraid it would." Her eyes filled with tears. "You as much as lied to me, and it's probably cost me my chance at being chief!"

My stomach turned over. "I'm sorry, really I am. I didn't mean to lie to you. I just couldn't bring Upton up again over dinner last night. But I'll fix things. Starting tonight."

We were alone on the path, so I started to take her hand. But she pulled it away and looked at me with fire in her eyes.

"You jerk, you still don't get it. The dean took you off the case. You're only here because Emily insisted. And I have to stay away from you. No tonight, no nothing between us anymore."

Her words hit me like a slap in the face. "Karen, after last night? You can't mean that!"

She looked down at the ground. "I'm afraid I do. Anything we started is over, at least until this case is behind us. I'm not risking my career for you."

She picked up her pace to pull in front of me, and I followed a few steps behind her until we reached the converted brownstone that housed student health. Emily was waiting for us in Dr. Stamford's office, sitting on an overstuffed couch with the psychiatrist seated in a rocking chair across from her. A coffee table between them held bottles of water and a box of tissues.

Dr. Stamford got up and offered her chair to Karen. "Grab that other chair across from my desk," she said to me. "I'll leave the three of you to talk."

Emily smiled weakly when Stamford left the office. "Thanks for coming over so quickly."

"Of course," Karen said. "Dr. Stamford told us things about that night were starting to come back to you. That's great—it could be a big step toward healing."

"I don't really remember very much. But all of sudden last night, I started to picture a man hulking over me."

"What did he do?" I asked.

She shuddered. "I think he pulled down my pants." Her eyes started to fill, and she looked away. "And then he stuck his fingers in me."

The tears started flowing, and Karen said, "Oh, Emily, I'm so sorry." She offered Emily the box of tissues and one of the bottles of water on the coffee table. Emily dried her eyes and blew her nose. She was quiet for a minute and then looked up again. "I'm okay now, thanks."

I was struck by how she pulled herself back together. This was one strong young woman. It hadn't been easy for her to tell us that.

Karen said, "I know it must be horrible for those memories to come back. But I have to ask, can you tell us anything about what the man looked like?"

Emily took a drink of water. "No, all I can picture is that he was big. It's like I was only half-conscious and just drifting in and out."

"Did you see his face? What he was wearing? Anything that might give us a clue."

Emily shook her head. "Nothing, I'm sorry. Just a big blob hulking over me. I'm sorry—I wish I could help."

Karen reached across the coffee table and took her hand. "Don't worry, just the fact that you can remember some of what happened helps us a lot. And it'll help you, too, as you work with Dr. Stamford."

Emily sniffled again and tried a weak smile. "Thanks."

"You may remember more in the next few days," Karen said. "A lot of date-rape drugs induce amnesia, but more memories may come back with time. Please let us know if that happens, okay? Any little details could help us figure out who did this to you."

"I will. Just one thing that I'm sure of—it wasn't Professor Upton."

"How do you know that?" I asked. "Was there something about the man that didn't look like Upton?"

"No," Emily said. "Like I told you, I didn't see him at all. Or at least I can't remember. But I'm sure it wasn't Steve. He'd never do that to me. Plus, he's been so supportive since it happened, letting me take time off and everything." She gave a wistful smile. "He was just thrilled when I told him I was starting to remember things. Like you, he said it was a big step toward healing."

———

Karen stopped to talk when we were out of the building. "I'll tell the dean that Emily can't give us anything in the way of identification yet, but she does remember being assaulted, and it's not unlikely that more will come back to her. I'm going to recommend that the dean wait and see before she has her meeting with Upton, but I'm not sure what she'll do. It's her call, and she's obviously anxious to get this over with."

I nodded. "And how about Emily's feeling that it wasn't Upton?"

She shrugged her shoulders. "Fine, I'll tell the dean that too. But Emily's conviction that it wasn't Upton isn't based on anything factual. Any more than your failure to recognize his guilt."

She turned on her heels and stomped off.

Leaving me wishing that I could just agree with her about Upton. And that I'd been open with her last night about yesterday's results being a collaboration with him.

And that I could follow her home.

14

I watched Karen disappear into the crowd of staffers leaving for the day. It was just after five, so these were the university employees with regular nine-to-five jobs. Administrators, maintenance workers, technicians, and so forth. The scientists, both faculty and students, didn't work such regular hours and would mostly still be at their desks or lab benches.

So what to make of the roller coaster Karen had me on? Roller coaster wasn't even the right word. It was more like some weird wave function that my colleagues in physics could derive, with oscillations continuously increasing in both amplitude and frequency. The abrupt change between last night's passion and today's rejection was as quick an up and down as I'd ever experienced. I had to admit I understood it. Karen's job was on the line, and my hesitancy in laying the blame on Upton was threatening her career. Not to mention my collaboration with him and the fact that I'd been too stupid to come clean with her. I could kick myself for that!

Okay, so I'd been a horse's ass not to say the results I was excited about last night were collaborative with Upton. But admitting that and understanding the pressures on Karen didn't make me feel much better. Nor did I care for the idea of twisting in the wind until the case somehow resolved.

I sighed audibly, and a young woman hurrying by looked at me as if she were the subject of my unwanted vocalization. All right, enough of standing here thinking about Karen. It was too early to go home, so I decided to return to the office. At least I could use the next hour or so to clear my desk of some of the routine paperwork that never stopped piling up.

Kristy was still there when I got to the office. "Burning the midnight oil?" I asked.

"Just trying to put together a couple more pieces of our search for the missing twenty thousand," she said. "But I'm surprised at what you've been up to. Do you guys really think Steve Upton assaulted one of our students?"

I jerked back in surprise. How could she know about that? Not from either Karen or me, I was sure. "What do you mean?" I asked.

She rolled her eyes. "Don't play dumb with me. I know about your meeting in Dean Houghton's office earlier. You guys think Upton assaulted Emily Jackson."

So that was it. A leak from the dean's office. I knew Kristy was close to the dean's administrative assistant, so I took a shot. "Ah, did Dede tell you about it?"

Her blush was confirmation enough. "That doesn't matter. But don't you realize it couldn't have been Upton?"

"Why do you say that?"

"He's gay. Why would he rape a woman?"

That was a new one on me. Although I'd never heard of Upton being involved with women, I hadn't thought of his being gay before.

"I'll bite," I said. "Why do you think he's gay? Another tidbit from your friend in the dean's office?"

"No, firsthand knowledge this time. Nancy and I ran into him at Sebastian's one night when we went out to celebrate our anniversary. He was with another man."

I frowned. "So what? Could have been a business dinner or whatever. Doesn't mean he's gay."

"You obviously don't know Sebastian's. It's a hangout for gay couples, both male and female. Upton was holding hands with his partner, and he came over to our table to chat after he spotted me looking at them. He's gay all right."

Interesting. Although I didn't think being gay ruled Upton out. Rape was an act of violence against women, not necessarily for sexual gratification.

"Thanks, that's important to know," I said. "I'll pass it on to the investigator handling the case. In the meantime, don't say anything about any of this, okay? I don't want things leaking from here like they seem to do from the dean's office."

"Of course, you know I don't gossip like Dede. Anyway, she said that Emily's starting to remember things, so you'll know the truth of what happened soon enough."

———

I thought about calling Karen with this news, but it didn't seem worth it. A call from me would only piss her off even more, and the revelation that Upton was gay wasn't urgent. The key was going to be what Emily could remember. If we were lucky, maybe enough would come back to her so that we could finally resolve what had really happened.

In the meantime, I tried to put the case out of my mind and tackled a couple hours' worth of meaningless paperwork. Then I headed home, picking up some sushi along the way.

By the time I'd had my usual drink, eaten, and walked Rosie, the lack of sleep from the night before hit me, and I zonked out on the couch in front of the TV. Only to be jolted awake by my phone ringing. I surfaced from a dream in which Karen had been about to pull the mask off a dark figure looming over her and looked at my watch. After midnight. Some kind of emergency?

I answered and felt a thrill of excitement when I heard Karen's voice. "We're downstairs and need to talk to you. Can you buzz us in?"

Suddenly I was wide awake. Had she reconsidered her earlier dismissal? "Of course, come on up."

I waited at the door for her to climb the stairs, ready to greet her with an embrace. But that dream was smashed when I saw that she wasn't alone. A tall, thin man dressed in a coat and tie was with her. She really had meant *we*. And the professional dress suggested that it was some kind of business call. In the middle of the night?

They reached my door, and Karen introduced her companion as Detective Farrell from the Boston police. "Can we come in and sit down?" she asked. "We have some news and need to talk to you."

That sounded ominous in the wee hours of the morning. I let them in and took a seat at one end of the couch I'd been sleeping on. Karen sat at the other end, and the detective pulled up a chair across from us.

I waited to see what merited a visit at this hour. Had Upton confessed? Or had Emily remembered something new?

Karen glanced questioningly at the detective. He nodded, and she licked her lips nervously. Then she turned to me. "Brad, I'm afraid we have bad news. Emily's dead."

It hit me like a punch in the stomach. The room started spinning, and I felt the bile rise in my throat.

"My God, what happened? She was fine this afternoon."

The detective answered. "I'm sorry. She was raped and murdered earlier this evening. We think around eight."

I tried to maintain control, but I couldn't. I ran to the bathroom and just made it to the toilet before I vomited. They mercifully left me alone, and I finally felt able to get up and wash my face. Then I breathed deeply for a minute and went back to the living room. It had stopped spinning.

"Sorry," I said. "I think I'll be okay now."

Karen reached over and touched my hand lightly. Nothing more than friendly support. "That's all right—we understand. It's a shock to have something like this happen to someone you know."

I nodded. "Do you know what happened?"

The detective answered. "She left the lab around seven thirty and was attacked in an alley on her way home. It was brutal. She was beaten, raped, and strangled. The medical examiner and crime-scene techs are going over everything now."

I closed my eyes and fought down the nausea again. Successfully this time. I turned to Karen. "Do you think this is related to the initial attack on her?"

"It has to be," Karen said. "It's too coincidental for this to happen right when she was starting to recover her memories of that night."

A chill came over me. It made sense, but there was a big gap. "So you think whoever assaulted her the first time killed her because she was starting to remember? But how would he have known that?"

Then I remembered what Emily had said about Upton. Just as Karen said, "Don't you remember? Emily told Upton she was starting to remember."

Another piece to add to the pile of circumstantial evidence placing the blame on Upton. "Yes, I do remember. That's what she said."

Karen said, "Right. And the only people who knew besides us were the dean, the lawyer, and Mike Singer. That solidifies Upton even further as the prime suspect. This time for murder. The cops are holding him now."

I shook my head. "I wouldn't be sure the list is so limited. The dean's office leaks gossip like a sieve. My administrative assistant even knew what was going on when I got back from our meeting with Emily."

Karen's eyes widened, and the detective said, "What the hell!"

I told them about my talk with Kristy. And that Upton was gay.

"So were you going to tell me about all this?" Karen asked with obvious annoyance.

I shrugged. "Of course, but there didn't seem to be any big rush."

She sighed. "You're right. It's not a big deal that Upton's gay. It certainly doesn't exclude him from something like this, although I guess it does make it statistically less likely. But the fact that Dede in the dean's office told your administrative assistant about Emily blows me away. God knows who else she told!"

The detective was scribbling in his notebook. He looked up with a scowl. "We'll interview her first thing tomorrow morning and find out. But if she's been a source of gossip about this, the news could have spread, and it'll be hard to limit our list of suspects."

Karen looked grim. "Shit! I'm going to have the dean can her for this. It's ridiculous. How about your assistant, Kristy? Did she tell anyone?"

"I really don't think so. I've never known her to be anything other than discreet. Go ahead and ask her about it, if you like. But in the meantime, you still think it was Upton who killed Emily?"

"He's certainly our prime suspect," the detective said. "He was top of the list for the initial assault, and he knew that Emily was starting to remember what happened that night. Meaning that he had plenty of motive to get rid of her before she remembered it was him. We've talked to him, and there's no firm alibi. Just says he was home watching TV."

"Even with the news leaking from the dean's office, it's hard to imagine that Derek heard Emily's memory was coming back," Karen added. "And just to be thorough, we checked out Mike Singer. He was at the lab, talked to some of his students, and was busy in his office as usual. We'll check with the students to be sure, but I've already verified his email activity."

The detective closed his notebook. "Bottom line is that Upton smells guilty as hell. We're hoping there's evidence at the crime scene that'll nail him. In the meantime, thanks for your help. We'll be in touch if we have any further questions." He got up, and Karen followed him to the door.

I watched them leave in silence. It made sense that Emily's initial assailant and her killer were one and the same. And it seemed all too likely that Emily had trusted Upton with the information that led to her own death.

A chill ran through me. Had I been defending a rapist and a murderer? Maybe I was just being too damned stupid to reach the obvious conclusion. Or too stubborn.

15

The dean called me into her office early the next morning. "You look like hell," she said.

So I guess a sleepless night showed. "Thanks. You do too," I replied.

She smiled grimly. "Yeah, it was a tough night. I guess for both of us. Do you want some coffee?"

She got up, and I followed her to a small kitchenette in the outer office, surprised that she was getting our coffees herself. Then it dawned on me. "No administrative assistant this morning?" I asked.

"I fired Dede earlier, after Karen and a Boston detective told me what happened."

"I'm sorry," I said.

"Don't be. I should have done it a long time ago. I knew she talked too much and let things leak out sometimes. But gossiping about this was too much."

She poured two mugs of coffee and added milk to hers. "Do you take anything in it?"

"No, just black." She handed me the mug, and I followed her back into her office.

"Do you know who Dede talked to?" I asked. "Was it just Kristy?"

She sighed and shook her head. "She swore she only talked to Kristy at first. But then the Boston cop leaned on her. Said it was a murder investigation, and she could be arrested for lying to the police. So all of a sudden, she remembered that she might have mentioned it to four or five other people. Like she was a damned broadcasting network!"

I rolled my eyes. "And who knows how many people each of them told, and so forth. So the bottom line is that a whole bunch of people knew that Emily's memory was coming back."

"The detective said they'd interview the people Dede told and start building up a list. But does it really matter? He told me that Upton heard it from Emily herself." She looked at me with a quizzical expression. "Don't tell me you still think it isn't him?"

The truth was that I found it even harder to imagine Upton as a murderer than as simply being guilty of a drunken sexual assault. And whatever Emily had told him about remembering that night, she obviously hadn't thought he was the guilty party. So why would he have been driven to kill her?

But I kept my answer neutral. No sense in provoking the dean's fury again. "I don't know anymore. I have to admit everything points to him, except my gut and the way Emily trusted him. Hopefully the investigation will turn up some solid evidence, and we'll be done speculating."

She steepled her hands in front of her. "I hope so. The cops apparently don't have enough to charge him at this point. And my hands are tied while he's under investigation, although the lawyers advised me to put him on paid leave and order him to stay away from campus. Which I did earlier this morning."

"Okay, that makes sense. I'll assign a couple of faculty members to serve as temporary advisors for his students."

"Good," she said. "And we also have some heavy pastoral work to do for the rest of your department. I'll get us together with the chaplain to come up with a strategy for that."

———

The news of Emily's death devastated the entire university community. The death of a student always does. In a large university like ours, accidents and even suicides sometimes happened. But murder was different. The horror of a young life cut short by an intentional act of violence permeated the campus. Students talked in hushed tones and no longer walked alone at night, suddenly afraid of what might be lurking in the dark.

The members of my own department were hardest hit, of course. Many of the faculty had taught Emily in their classrooms. Others had been on her thesis advisory committee or attended her departmental seminars. And the students were shocked and dismayed by the loss of a colleague many of them had studied or worked with. Not to mention those who had been Emily's lab mates or friends.

The university chaplain and the dean helped me lead the department through it. The chaplain and I held separate meetings for faculty, students, and staff to talk about the grief process, as well as about safety precautions. The dean made a bevy of grief counselors available full time, and the university police put on extra details that gave everyone at least some sense of security.

The dean and I met Emily's parents at the airport when they arrived from Chicago and did our best to make them comfortable. They held themselves together with a quiet strength, much like Emily herself had displayed. The body would be returned to Chicago for private burial once the medical examiner was finished, but the dean arranged for a university-wide memorial service to be held a week after Emily's death.

The service took place in the large Gothic chapel that was the university's official center of worship. All three-hundred-plus seats were filled for the memorial. Both of Emily's parents broke down as they spoke but bravely managed to get through their remarks. They were followed by her older brother, a lawyer from New York, who recounted her childhood interest in science. Then Emily's friend Carol went to the podium. She tried, but she couldn't make it through her speech, eventually breaking down in tears and being helped from the stage by the chaplain.

The last speaker was Mike Singer, whom the dean had asked to represent the faculty in place of Upton. He began by painting an eloquent picture of Emily as a brilliant student and rising star, whose life had been tragically cut short but whose work would live on in the scientific contributions she'd made. Unfortunately, he couldn't resist the temptation to shift his focus and transition to talking about how important her work with him on Immunoboost was going to be. I could feel the audience grow restless as he dwelled on what amounted to his own accomplishments rather than on Emily's. It was in ridiculously poor taste, but I wasn't surprised that Singer was unable to resist an opportunity for self-promotion. Finally he stopped, and the chaplain concluded the service by inviting the audience to a reception in the large meeting hall adjacent to the chapel.

I spotted Karen maybe a dozen people ahead of me in the line of mourners waiting to pay their respects to the family. My stomach tingled as I watched her slowly moving forward. I couldn't keep my eyes away from the soft skin on the back of her neck. Or stop my imagination from envisioning the rest of her naked body. Had it only been a week ago? And where did things stand now?

She reached the end of the line, paid her respects, and moved on. I lost sight of her by the time I made it through and thought she'd already left. But then I spotted her loading her plate at a large buffet table in the back. Maybe it was another one of those days when she hadn't had time for lunch.

I made my way over to her. I wasn't sure I'd be welcome, but I couldn't resist the opportunity to try to talk to her. Maybe I could fall on my knees and beg her forgiveness. Or something.

She spotted me and gave me a half smile, which I took as at least modest encouragement. "How're you doing?" she asked. "This must be pretty traumatic for your department."

Not exactly an emotion-packed greeting, but at least it was welcoming. "Traumatic is right," I said. "Although people are starting to calm down now. The chaplain and grief counselors have helped a lot."

"Yeah, they're good at what they do. Unfortunately, they've had lots of practice. This memorial will probably help too. I thought it was nice, except for Singer being an asshole."

I chuckled softly. "Yes, he did go a bit overboard." She seemed friendly, maybe even glad to see me. Or was that just the hopeful side of my imagination? I decided to risk it. "Karen, do you think we could have dinner again? Or something?"

She gave me a slow smile but with real warmth. "Yes, I'd like that. But we still have to wait until the case is finished. Especially with the decision on the new chief of detectives hanging in the balance." She touched my arm lightly. Nothing that would be embarrassing to anyone looking on, but a gesture that said a lot. "Can you hold out?"

An enormous sense of relief washed over me. So there was hope after all. "Yes, I can hold out. Whatever it takes. How're things on the case going?"

"Slow. Upton's hired a lawyer, and there isn't enough to arrest him. Especially since the word about Emily leaked out, we need something solid. But the detectives are busy working on crime-scene evidence and trying to find somebody who saw something that night."

"No breaks?"

She hesitated. "I probably shouldn't tell you this, but they found a broken yardstick in a dumpster a block away from the alley where she was killed. It was covered with blood, and they think it was used for the rape. Lots of Emily's DNA, but so far, that's it. Nothing from anybody else. Although they're still analyzing samples."

"Do you think they might find something more?"

"I don't know. There's always a possibility. But there was one other interesting thing. It wasn't an ordinary yardstick. It was a special, heavy-duty kind. Which turns out to be the kind of yardstick the university orders in bulk for use as pointers in lecture halls and faculty offices."

I knew just what she meant. I had one in my office. And Josh had used one in Upton's office when we met there to discuss his and Laurie's project last week. The day before Emily was killed.

16

It took a couple of weeks, but the department gradually returned to normal. Except that the women no longer walked home alone at night.

I hadn't heard from Karen since the memorial service, so I assumed that the investigation was continuing without notable progress. Or that I'd misread her at the service, and Karen had no interest in rekindling our relationship. Or both.

I didn't know what to make of her anymore. The thrill of our night together followed by her turnabout the next day. Then renewed hope at the memorial. And now silence. I understood the conflict between her job and our relationship, but this all seemed like the kind of ups and downs I was too old for. Only one thing was clear—if anything was going to happen between us, it would have to wait until the case was settled. I tried to put Karen on hold in a back corner of my mind until then. With only partial success.

On the other hand, work in the lab was moving forward, particularly Laurie's collaboration with Josh. One of the new compounds he'd synthesized turned out to be even more effective than the previous version, and Laurie had shown that it worked against several different kinds of cancer cells—breast, colon, brain, and prostate—in addition to the lung cancer she'd first tried it on. And even more exciting, it worked with chemotherapeutic drugs as well as irradiation. Big news, but now the question was, What to do next? Both Laurie and Josh wanted to make some more derivatives, but this was going to require more sophisticated chemistry than Josh could handle without help.

In Upton's absence, there weren't any full-time chemists in the department. Singer was closest. He was always saying how useful his chemistry background was in collaborating with Upton. So when Upton was put on leave, I talked Singer into taking on the role of advisor to most of Upton's students, including Josh. It hadn't been easy to get him to accept the extra work, but I cajoled him into it by saying that he was really the only qualified member of the department to supervise students engaged in synthetic chemistry. Blatant as it was, the flattery worked.

Which meant that now I needed to set up a meeting with Singer for Laurie, Josh, and myself. It took a lengthy exchange of emails, but he finally found an opening in his schedule. After he took pains to point out that he didn't think Josh and Laurie's project was worthwhile and that he'd prefer to reassign Josh to work on one of his own projects instead of something that Upton had originated. Rather obnoxiously, he sent those emails not just to me but also to the students.

After all that, none of us particularly looked forward to talking with him. Nonetheless, when the time arrived for the scheduled meeting, Laurie, Josh, and I met outside Singer's office. The door was closed, so I knocked. No answer. I tried again, still without a response. I shrugged my shoulders. "He'll be here. Let's just wait."

It took less than five minutes before Laurie proclaimed, "He's an asshole. Let's go."

"No, c'mon," I said. "It was hard enough to arrange this. Just hang on."

Fortunately, Josh seconded my request. "Yeah, hold on, Laurie. He may be an asshole, but we need his help."

We waited. And waited. Until Singer finally got off the elevator and lumbered down the hall toward us—fifteen minutes after our scheduled meeting time.

He unlocked his office door without an apology. "All right, let's get going. What is it that I can do for you?"

I tried to establish an atmosphere of cooperation as we took seats at his conference table. "Thanks for meeting with us. As you know, Laurie and Josh have some interesting results with a series of compounds Josh has made. We think the next step is to synthesize some additional derivatives, but we just don't have the chemistry background to know what's possible or how to go about it. That's the part of the project where Upton was key, and we're hoping you can step in and give us a hand. Of course, with full acknowledgment of your efforts by coauthorship when we publish."

Singer nodded, apparently satisfied with the bait of authorship. "Sure, I can help you with synthesis. Show me what you're after."

"Can I use PowerPoint?" Josh asked.

Singer nodded toward a projector on his table, and Josh hooked up the laptop he'd brought with him. His first slide showed the compounds they'd tested so far with a summary of the key results with each.

"As you can see, this last derivative I made is significantly more effective than the starting compound," Josh said.

He was pointing to the structures with his hand, and his back blocked my view of the screen. "Josh, could you use a pointer and stand to the side? I'm sorry, but I can't see through you."

"Of course, sorry." He looked under the screen and got a pointer. The same kind that had been used on Emily. Then he showed me the structures again and moved on to the next slide. "Based on our results so far, I'd like to synthesize these two derivatives for further testing. You see that they have methyl and ethyl groups in place of the bromo group we have in our current compound. But this isn't a simple reaction, and I need some help with the synthesis."

Singer nodded. "Yes, that sounds like a good thing to try. How do you think you'd go about making those compounds?"

Josh looked perplexed. "I'm afraid I have no idea. I don't know that kind of chemistry."

"And you were Upton's student?" Singer scoffed. "You should figure out a plan for the synthesis yourself, not just ask me about it. You're supposed to be a graduate student, learning to be an independent scientist."

I sat up with a start. This was the kind of bullying some faculty members liked to use on their students. Show them who's boss. It was stupid and inappropriate and decidedly not the kind of behavior I expected in my department.

Josh looked embarrassed. "I'm sorry, but it really isn't my field. I've tried to research it, but I need some guidance on the best approach."

Singer raised his right eyebrow. "That's ridiculous. Go do your homework, and come back when you have a proposal for me to look at."

That was too much. I started to protest, but suddenly Laurie spoke up. "Oh wait, couldn't we use a modified Schwinn reaction?"

Josh looked at her openmouthed, and Singer smiled. "Finally, somebody who knows some chemistry. I'm glad to see that at least one of the students working on this has some initiative. Let's meet again after you give that a try and see how it works. Then I can give you more specific advice on how to tweak things to improve your yield."

Laurie said it would probably take a couple of weeks to do the initial reactions, and we left. Once the three of us were out in the hall, I turned to her. "That was great, but where did it come from? I didn't know you had any chemistry background."

"Neither did I," Josh said.

She smiled sweetly at us. "I don't know any chemistry. There's no such thing as a Schwinn reaction. I made it up. Schwinn is just the kind of bike I ride. That man is such a jerk, giving Josh shit when he doesn't know anything himself."

Josh broke into a fit of laughter, which Laurie quickly joined. I restrained myself with a smile and shake of my head. This was a new side of Mike Singer. Not just arrogant, but a bully. And a useless one, at least as far as chemistry was concerned.

———

I was still laughing to myself all the way back to my office. What a pompous ass! I wondered how long it would take Singer to figure out that Laurie had made a fool of him. I'd like to be a fly on the wall when he realized what had happened.

Kristy looked up and smiled when I entered the office. "You look like you're in a good mood. Maybe this is a good time to talk about the financial stuff I've been working on."

"You mean the missing twenty thousand? Sure, why not. Have you made progress?"

She picked up some papers and followed me into my office.

"I have, with Ed Carlson's help. We've been able to trace the problem to three research accounts, from which the auditors have questioned whether some reimbursement requests are appropriate."

"What do you mean? What kind of questions?"

"They're mostly consulting fees to a woman from another institution, and the question is whether they can allowably be charged to our grants. She's not listed as personnel on the grants, and the auditors say these are the kind of charges that typically come up when someone is using government funds to give presents to a girlfriend."

I knew that the misuse of grant funds was a fairly common form of misconduct among scientists. But it was also something that I found abhorrent. "God, really? Whose grants are they?"

"They're all big, multi-investigator grants, with a dozen or more faculty members on each. So it's not clear who's involved. But I do know the name of the woman in question. Sally Lipton, from Yale. Ed suggested that maybe you could research her science and figure out which of our faculty members she might be collaborating with."

"It's possible," I said. "Give me the three grant numbers and the names of the faculty members on each of them. I'll look up Sally Lipton and see if I can make a connection."

Kristy handed me a sheet of paper. "I figured that's what you'd need. Here you go."

———

I started by pulling up information on the three grants from our department database. All three were big program project grants that funded collaborations between biologists and chemists under the umbrella of chemical biology. It was a hot area of interdisciplinary research that targeted the development of new drugs or other chemicals that were useful for biological investigations—everything from drugs to treat cancer to new dyes for studying cells in the microscope. About half of the faculty involved were in my department. I was on two of the grants myself, and four of our faculty members were on all three: Steve Upton, Mike Singer, and two others who were heavily into drug development. Presumably it was one of those four who was tied to Sally Lipton.

As Kristy had indicated, none of the grants listed Sally Lipton as either an investigator or a collaborator. That didn't necessarily mean that she wasn't working with one or more of our faculty members on the projects, but it certainly explained why payments to her from these accounts looked suspicious to an auditor.

Next, I googled Sally Lipton at Yale. That brought up her website in the Department of Chemistry. She was working in the general area of drug design, which made sense in terms of her involvement as a potential collaborator on our projects. But there were no joint publications with any of our faculty members in the list of her papers, which covered the last five years.

That didn't look good for an active collaboration, but maybe there were some older papers that would at least explain a connection. I went into PubMed, the National Library of Medicine's database of scientific publications. Searching there for Sally Lipton brought up almost a hundred papers published over the last fifteen years. Then I searched her publications for each of my four faculty members as coauthors. Success. She had three papers coauthored with Mike Singer, published between ten and twelve years ago.

Full copies of Lipton's papers with Singer were available online, and I pulled them up for a closer look. Interestingly, the only institution listed in the bylines was Yale. Then I remembered. We'd recruited Singer to BTI from Yale somewhere around ten years ago, before I was chair of the department. It looked like he had known and worked with Lipton while he was a faculty member at Yale. Maybe they were continuing their collaboration, but there was no evidence of ongoing work between them. That made it hard to discount the possibility that they'd developed and maintained a more intimate kind of relationship.

I had one more window back to Singer's years at Yale. His personnel file would contain all the details of his recruitment here, including references from his former colleagues at Yale, as well as correspondence related to his status in the field, such as nominations for awards and prizes. Would any of those letters be written by Lipton or refer to the two of them?

I got up and went to the filing cabinet that contained confidential personnel files for all the department's faculty members. Singer's was thicker than most, which was no surprise, given his stature and seniority. It was going to take more than a quick read to get through it.

I started at the front of the file, with the most recent material. I'd seen everything that had come in over the last few years, since I'd been chair, so I scanned that quickly. There were lots of letters with glowing reports of Singer's accomplishments and considerable reputation. But nothing from or about Sally Lipton.

Then I had to slow down as I worked back in time, but it was more of the same. Accolades from around the world, supporting him for various awards and honors. But nothing that mentioned Sally Lipton. Half an hour later, I made it back to the beginning, when we had recruited Singer from Yale.

And then it stopped making sense. He was already a major player in his field when we got him here, and his recruitment had been a big deal. There were a dozen or so letters from faculty members at leading universities testifying to his accomplishments. And lengthy correspondence between Singer and Richard Solomon, chair of the department at the time, regarding the terms of Singer's appointment. Singer had demanded a high salary, lots of lab space, and a substantial amount of discretionary money from the university that he could use for supplies, equipment, and research personnel in his lab. It was a protracted negotiation, with Solomon making offers and Singer replying that Yale had already countered with better terms that BTI now had to match. Nothing unusual there. That was the way negotiations with star faculty went, although this was a bit tackier than most.

But as I looked through it, I realized there was a big piece missing. There were no copies of the counteroffers from Yale that Singer repeatedly referred to, just his statements of what they were. That was bizarre. We *always* required copies of counteroffers from the candidate's current institution in a negotiation like this. Trust but verify was a firm policy of the BTI administration. Yet there was nothing here to indicate that Yale was trying to keep him.

And then I realized it went even deeper. There was nothing from *anyone* at Yale about him in the file. No recommendations from colleagues, no praise from administrators, no comments from his department chair. Just nothing. As if his departure was shrouded in official silence.

The only times I knew something like this to happen were when faculty members left their institutions under a cloud. Either on bad terms with their home departments or as a resolution to some kind of misconduct dispute, typically with a nondisclosure agreement in place. Meaning Singer had probably been bluffing about Yale's efforts to retain him, and we had been suckered into meeting nonexistent counteroffers. And more important, it looked like something had gone sour for him at his previous institution.

I needed to figure this out. If Singer had been involved in some kind of problem at Yale, it could come back to bite us by compromising the credibility of his testimony against Upton. Of course, it could have been just an angry disagreement with his department chair about space or resources. But it was also possible that he'd been under investigation for some kind of misconduct. Judging from the way he'd treated Josh, he could easily have gotten into trouble for harassing his students. That wouldn't be so bad for us, but I had an uneasy feeling that he could have been involved in the same kind of financial fraud that seemed to be going on here. And was Sally Lipton some-how involved—both then and now?

It seemed unlikely that official inquiries would get anywhere, but I knew a few people at Yale, including Martin Dawson, an old friend who was now chair of Singer's former department. I thought of talking to him by phone but decided against it. As Karen had taught me, a personal touch would be better. And New Haven was just two and a half hours away.

I confirmed by email that Martin would be available tomor-row for lunch. And maybe I'd also pay a surprise visit to the mystery woman, Sally Lipton.

17

I took I-95 down to New Haven. Not the fastest route, but the final portion was along the coast, and I always enjoyed the sight and smell of the ocean. When I got to Old Saybrook, about thirty miles from my destination, I pulled off the highway and found an oceanside café where I stopped for coffee and a homemade donut on the patio. I always preferred honey dip, but they had some raspberry jellies that looked really good. I considered the matter carefully and was forced to settle on one of each. I wasn't sure what my schedule would be like once I got to Yale, so I figured that I might as well enjoy what was turning out to be a bright, sunny day, still warm enough to sit outdoors.

I planned to start by talking to Martin Dawson. I'd known Martin since graduate school, and he was a good guy. More important, as chair of the Department of Molecular, Cellular, and Developmental Biology, he'd have access to whatever personnel files pertained to Singer's departure. His email response had been enthusiastic when I proposed a visit, and I didn't think he'd be reluctant to share what he knew. Or could find out.

Martin's office was on the twelfth floor of the Kline Biology Tower, a sixteen-story building that was easy to find because it was the tallest on campus. I identified myself as an old friend of Martin's to an administrative assistant in the outer office and said that Martin was expecting me. She looked at me dubiously and said she wasn't aware of an appointment and would have to check with Professor Dawson. She knocked on his door and went into Martin's office, only to be followed moments later by Martin himself, bursting through the door and grabbing my hand with his characteristic exuberance.

"Brad, how good to see you! It's been what, at least two years now? Let's go get some lunch and catch up."

We took the elevator down and walked a few blocks to a deli on Chapel Street. There were a handful of tables outside, two of them still empty because it wasn't quite noon, and we grabbed one.

"Great place," Martin said. "Best Reubens in the world. So how are you doing in the never-ending struggle to be department chair and still run your lab?"

"Probably about as well as you are," I said.

We exchanged jokes about the life of a chair, which we both agreed was not anything that we'd been prepared for, by either education or experience. The waitress came by with menus, but Martin waved them away. "We don't need those. I'll have a Reuben. You too. Right, Brad?"

I laughed. "Of course. Couldn't pass up the world's best."

"So how about research, Brad? Can you still get anything done in your lab?"

"Actually, I've gotten lucky with one of my students." I told him about the work Laurie was doing with Josh as the waitress brought our sandwiches.

"Fabulous," he said. "Our students can be our saviors. And this in the middle of one of your students having been murdered just a few weeks ago. That must be horrible for you to deal with."

I fell serious. "It is. There's no way to describe it. Things are sort of back to normal in the department, but there's a pall hanging over everyone. And the police are still working on the case."

"I'm so sorry. But eat, eat. Don't let your sandwich get cold."

I took a big bite. It really was good. "You're right, best in the world."

"Good, enjoy. But tell me, to what do I owe this visit? You and I are both too busy for simple pleasures."

"You're right—I do have an ulterior motive. What can you tell me about Mike Singer? In particular, about the circumstances of his leaving here to join our department at BTI?"

He raised his eyebrows. "And you're curious because . . .? Is he being some sort of problem for you?"

"I'm not sure," I said honestly. "I had occasion to look through his file and was struck that there's nothing in it from anyone at Yale. No recommendations, no documentation of counteroffers during his recruitment, nothing. It made me wonder if he left here under some sort of a cloud."

Martin leaned back and rubbed his chin. A gesture that I knew meant he was thinking. "He left several years before I became chair, so I don't know the details. I do remember that my colleagues and I were surprised. He went on leave, and then he never came back, moving to your place instead. I had assumed he was working with somebody in your department during his leave and decided to stay."

"No, he wasn't with us before he joined the department full time. Do you have his file in your office? Maybe there's more information in there."

"Sorry, I only have the files of active members of the department. Since Singer's gone, all of his stuff would be archived in the college storage."

"Can I get in to take a look at it?"

"Only with permission from the dean. Why is this so important? He was here, and now he's gone. Lots of faculty members move between institutions."

"Look, can you keep this confidential?" He nodded, and I continued. "Our auditors are questioning expenses associated with some of his grants, involving consulting fees paid to a woman in your chemistry department. It made me want to check his connections back here, and I'm flummoxed by the absence of history in his file. I'd like to find out what went on before he joined us, especially to see if there are any problems or connections with the woman from his years here."

Martin turned pale as I talked. "You don't think he's associated with your murder case, do you?"

"No, no. Nothing like that. Just some financial irregularities—but enough that I need to look into it."

His color returned as he frowned and then nodded. "All right, I'll try to help you. What are you doing for dinner tonight?"

"I don't know. Probably just grab some takeout after I get home and eat in my condo. Why?"

"Let me invite you to stay in New Haven tonight and have dinner with me. We can go to the original Pepe's pizza, an exceptional treat for a Bostonian. Check yourself into a hotel and meet me there at seven. I'll arrange an interesting field trip for you afterward."

I found a hotel and called my downstairs neighbor to make overnight arrangements for Rosie. Then, with the afternoon free, I decided to pay Sally Lipton a visit. Googling her in preparation for the meeting revealed an odd history. She had come to Yale as an assistant professor fifteen years ago. Tenure track, meaning that after seven years, she'd be evaluated for promotion to a tenured position. If the tenure evaluation was successful, she'd be promoted to associate and then full professor. If she was denied tenure, she'd have to leave. But now her rank was listed as *research* professor, which meant she wasn't tenured and was only allowed to stay on a temporary basis as long as she could bring in grants to support her own salary.

The whole thing didn't make sense. Yale, like most major universities, had a firm up-or-out tenure policy. When the time for tenure evaluation came, the candidate was either granted tenure or forced to leave the university. Staying on in a second-tier, nontenured position was not an option. Yet that seemed to be exactly what Sally Lipton was doing.

I found her office on the third floor of the Chemistry Research Building. The door was slightly ajar, so I knocked and was greeted by a terse, "Yes, come in."

The woman behind the desk looked older than her age, which I figured to be early forties from her academic record. She peered at me through heavy, black-framed glasses, set on a narrow face beneath close-cropped, graying brown hair. "What do you want?"

I introduced myself and took one of the chairs across from her desk. "If you have a minute, I'd like to talk to you about your work with Mike Singer. As you know, he's a member of my department, and I've noticed your collaboration with him on some of his grants. I'm visiting Yale today and found myself with some free time this afternoon, so I thought I'd take the opportunity to stop by and meet you."

"Yes, I know Singer. I do a little consulting for him. What's to talk about?"

"I'm just curious. How long have the two of you worked together?"

"We met shortly after I came here as a new assistant professor, maybe fifteen years ago. We did some things together when I first got my lab set up, published a couple of joint papers."

"And you continued consulting on his projects after he left," I said. "His departure must have been a blow to you and your colleagues in chemistry. What made him move to my place?"

She swiveled her chair around to look at me face on. "What makes anyone move? A better offer, I guess. I really don't know the details." She looked pointedly at her watch. "Is there anything else I can do for you? If not, I have to prepare for my class in an hour."

She turned back to her computer before I even had a chance to get up.

———

The original Pepe's was on Wooster Street, about a mile from my hotel. Martin was waiting when I got there and eagerly pointed out the original coal-fired oven as we were shown to our table. We ordered two medium pizzas—a pepperoni and Pepe's specialty, a white clam—along with a pitcher of Sam Adams. The beer came immediately, the pizzas soon after, and Martin tucked in as if lunch was no more than a distant memory. I did my best to keep up.

When I saw Martin look longingly at the last piece of white clam, I threw in the towel.

"Go ahead," I said. "I'm stuffed."

He gave an exaggerated shrug. "If I must. Can't waste Pepe's specialty. Best pizza in the world, right?"

I poured myself a fresh glass from our pitcher of Sam Adams. "That's what you said about our sandwiches at lunch too. Is all the food in New Haven the best in the world? You know Pepe's recently opened a place in Boston, right?"

He gave me a self-satisfied smile. "Everywhere I go is the best, absolutely. And the Boston place can't hold a candle to this. Been here since 1925. The best—"

I held up my hands in the universal gesture of surrender. "Okay, the best in the world. I won't argue. But other than enjoying your company and the eats, this trip hasn't been very productive. You said you had something interesting planned after dinner?"

He reached into his pocket, pulled out a key ring, and jangled it at me. "I do. And it's after nine, so we can get going any time now." He finished his pizza, took a look at the check, and put cash down on the table. "No records of tonight's adventure left behind."

We drove to campus, and Martin parked in the biology building lot. "Figured we'd park in my usual place and then walk over to our destination," he explained.

The administration building was a large brick building about two blocks away. In contrast to the biology building, which still had several lighted windows at nine thirty, the administration building was completely dark.

"Good," Martin said. "Our administrators are solid nine-to-fivers."

He took out the keychain and unlocked the front door. "A loan from a friend of mine in the dean's office. I told her I needed to check an old file and didn't have time to get over here during normal business hours."

"I take it that it's not legit for us to be here?"

"It's not, but I don't think we'll be bothered." He led the way down a staircase to the basement. Then he used another borrowed key, and we entered a cavernous room filled with rows and rows of filing cabinets.

"Voilà," he said. "Welcome to the Yale faculty mausoleum."

It was completely dark, and we used the flashlights on our phones to read the labels on the filing cabinet drawers. They were carefully alphabetized, and we found a drawer labeled *Silver-Snodgrass* toward the back of the room. Mike Singer's file was right where it should be. So far, so good.

But suddenly the lights came on, and a voice from the front of the room called out, "Hello. Who's there?"

I was paralyzed, but Martin moved quickly. "Duck down out of sight and stay put," he whispered in my ear. "I'll handle this. Then you get back to your hotel afterward."

I crouched down as Martin went out into the aisle. "Hello, what's up? I'm just looking for an old file," he said.

He moved out of my line of sight, and I heard the interloper walk over toward him.

"Security. Do you have some identification?"

"Of course. I'm Professor Dawson, chair of the Department of Molecular, Cellular, and Developmental Biology."

There was a pause, during which I assumed the security guy checked Martin's ID. "Okay. Do you have authorization to be in here? I was doing rounds and saw a light."

Martin was unfazed. "Yes, Mary Cartwright in the dean's office lent me her keys. As I said, I just had to do a quick check of an old personnel file. I'm sorry to have bothered you. Here, let's go, and I'll buy you a beer for your trouble."

I peeked around the corner to see Martin take something out of his wallet and hand it to the guard. No doubt it was worth more than a beer.

The guard started to say, "I can't accept——"

But Martin put his arm around the guard's shoulders and cut him off. "What are you talking about? Just a friendly beer. Who could object to that?"

I could almost hear the guard smile. "Well, okay. Thank you, Professor. If you're finished, can I show you out?"

"Sure," Martin said. "I'm all set."

I heard them walk away. Then the lights went out, and the door closed. Martin seemed to have successfully talked and bribed his way out of it. The old Martin charm had been his forte since graduate school.

I waited a few minutes and then turned my attention back to Singer's file. The papers in it were chronologically arranged, so I went to the back, looking for correspondence about his departure. What I found was a nondisclosure agreement binding the signatories to confidentiality concerning the circumstances of Singer's resignation from the university.

It was signed by Mike Singer and four other people, including a couple whose names I recognized. One of them made my heart beat faster.

Sally Lipton.

18

I got lost twice on the way back to my hotel. Partly because of my usual bad sense of direction and partly because my mind was focused on Singer's nondisclosure agreement. It was after eleven when I made it back to my room and looked at a text from Martin.

Trust you made it back okay. Hope you found what you needed.

I didn't want to tell him what I'd found. No sense involving him any more than necessary. So I just sent a quick reply. *Yes, back in hotel now. Interesting venture, thanks! Owe you dinner next time you're in Boston.*

He must have been waiting to hear from me. His response was immediate. And as usual, centered on food. *You're welcome. Any decent restaurants there?*

I laughed out loud in a release of the evening's tension. Mixed in with relief that Martin wasn't going to press me for more information. *Take you to the original Regina's pizza in the North End. Put it up against your Pepe's for the world's best any day! Wanna bet the amount you bribed the security guard?*

I could almost hear the snort of derision in his response. *Hah! You're on. See you soon.*

I needed to get some sleep before the drive back to Boston tomorrow. But I couldn't do it yet. I was too blown away by the discovery that Singer's departure from Yale was veiled in secrecy. With Sally Lipton somehow involved.

There could, of course, be several reasons for a nondisclosure agreement. Singer was a highflier, and Yale might have bent over backward to keep him from leaving. If so, they may very well have made him an offer that was so rich they wouldn't want other faculty members to know about it. That would explain an agreement between Singer and the Yale administrators who had signed on. But why Sally Lipton?

Alternatively, Singer had left Yale under a cloud. Perhaps involving the same kind of financial shenanigans that he might be implicated in at BTI. If so, Lipton's signature implied that she was involved. Both then and now.

In addition to Singer and Sally Lipton, the agreement was signed by the dean of Yale's Faculty of Arts and Sciences and the president of Yale University. As well as by someone named Martha Daniels, who didn't have an official title.

I knew the former dean, Kenneth Emerson. He was now president of my own university, having moved to the top position at BTI a year or so after Singer joined us. In fact, if I remembered correctly, Singer had been a member of the search committee that had selected Emerson for the top job, suggesting that whatever had happened to Singer at Yale hadn't bothered Emerson. Interesting, but it wasn't going to help me find out anything more. Emerson would hardly break a nondisclosure agreement to talk to me about it. Nor would the Yale president.

Seeing Sally Lipton's name on the agreement told me a lot. It meant there was a tie between her and Singer going way back and including some involvement in—or at least knowledge of— the details of his departure from Yale. But based on my interaction with her this afternoon, it wasn't something she was going to talk to me about.

So that left one other possibility to look into. The other unidentified signatory, Martha Daniels. I revved up my laptop and searched for her in PubMed. I came up with two published papers from ten years ago, about the time Singer left Yale. The footnotes indicated that Martha Daniels had been a graduate student in chemistry. Neither Singer nor Sally Lipton was a co-author on either of the papers, so neither appeared to have been directly involved with her work.

The most recent of the two papers said that the research had been part of Martha's PhD thesis, implying that she'd graduated from Yale with a PhD in chemistry and two publications in first-rate journals to her name. Those were strong credentials, and I would have expected her to go on to a position at a leading research university. But there was nothing more recent from her in the published literature, meaning that she hadn't pursued an active research career.

I switched to Google. It took some digging, but I managed to find her listed as a junior faculty member at Farmington Community College the year after she presumably graduated. I had to google Farmington to identify it as a small community college in the Lakes Region of New Hampshire. Not the kind of prestigious place I'd have expected a PhD from Yale to wind up at. But maybe Martha had been more interested in teaching than in research. And who knows, maybe she had family in New Hampshire.

The current Farmington website didn't show her listed as faculty, so I did more searching until I found a Farmington archive. She'd been a faculty member at Farmington for only two years, eight and nine years ago. And then she just wasn't there anymore. No indication of a forwarding address at another college or university.

Farmington was in Holderness, so I tried googling "Martha Daniels Holderness New Hampshire." That brought up an old article from the *Holderness Gazette*, reporting that Martha Daniels had committed suicide by hanging herself.

I felt a shiver go down my spine as I stared at the newspaper article. What had driven a young woman like this to take her own life? Was she depressed by a career situation so different from what she'd apparently been pursuing at Yale? And was that somehow tied to her involvement with Mike Singer in whatever the nondisclosure agreement was about?

I needed to find out more about Martha. Maybe talk to someone who knew her and could shed some light on whatever had happened. The obvious starting point was the cops who had investigated her death, but I didn't think they'd talk to me. But I knew someone they would open up to.

I texted Karen, being purposefully vague.

I've been looking into an irregularity involving Mike Singer's grants and need your help in sorting things out. It has nothing to do with Upton or Emily, so no conflict. Can we meet for coffee or lunch?

It was too late for her to answer, but she'd get it in the morning and hopefully be intrigued enough to meet. In the meantime, I was too charged with adrenaline to sleep, so I checked out of the hotel and headed back to Boston. At least the traffic would be light at two in the morning.

19

I awoke to the noise of blaring horns outside my bedroom window. A downside of living on a main thoroughfare in downtown Boston. The clock said it was almost eight. Driving back from New Haven last night hadn't been the greatest idea. My adrenaline high had lasted about an hour. After that, I'd fought to stay awake until I finally got to my condo and collapsed in bed. And now, after less than five hours of sleep, I had to drag myself up again.

I shuffled into the kitchen and made twice my usual amount of coffee, assuming that caffeine would help. Then I looked at my phone. There was a text from Karen, which revitalized me more than I hoped the coffee would.

Can meet later today, as long as this isn't about Steve Upton. Still can't talk to you about that. But if it's something else, how about eleven o'clock at Tessa's?

I gave myself a mental high five. Not only would I get Karen's help, but I'd also have a chance to see her again. I wrote back.

Not about Upton, I promise. Meet you there and then. I hesitated and then added, *Looking forward to seeing you again.*

She answered immediately, and I felt a jolt of pleasure when I read her response: *Me too!*

———

Tessa's was a small bakery/coffeehouse across the street from Karen's office in the university police headquarters. She was waiting at a back table when I got there, so I picked up a cup of coffee from the counter and sat across from her. She looked up at me with moist eyes and a smile that gave me butterflies.

"It's been a while," she said. "How've you been?"

I'd intended to keep this professional, but the warmth in her eyes fractured that resolve. I reached across the table and squeezed her hand. "Okay, except that I've missed you."

"I've missed you too. I'm sorry—I really haven't had any other choice. The dean was furious about what happened between you and Upton, and her orders for me to stay away from you were quite clear."

"I understand. I'm sorry I got you messed up in that. But it's okay for us to talk now?"

She nodded. "I think so. You promised it wasn't about Upton, and I'm afraid his case isn't going anywhere anyway."

I raised my eyebrows. "That doesn't sound very good. Can you tell me what's happened?"

She shrugged. "I guess. Mostly it's what hasn't happened. The cops haven't found any physical evidence linking him to Emily's murder, and it turns out that he has a plausible alibi after all. After some heavy questioning, he told the detectives that he's gay and was at home watching a movie with his boyfriend. It's not perfect, but the boyfriend swears to it, the movie was rented from Amazon when he says it was, and the GPSs on both their phones were at

Upton's house. He obviously could have set the movie and the phones up and gotten his boyfriend to lie, but in the absence of anything linking him to the crime scene, the cops don't have any evidence to pursue charges. So they've put him on the back burner and are trying to dig up other suspects—but without success."

"Wow. So what's going to happen to Upton? You still think he's guilty, right?"

"I do. But thinking isn't the same as proving it. The dean's going to go ahead and terminate him with a negotiated nondisclosure agreement like we talked about earlier, so at least we'll be rid of him. But the son of a bitch is going to be free to find another job elsewhere."

"And if you're right, he'll have gotten away with murder."

She frowned. "The investigation's still open, so there's nothing to preclude the cops finding what they need and arresting him at any point in the future. But for now, yes. Anyway, I've said too much. We weren't supposed to talk about Upton, remember?"

I nodded. "Right, sorry. I wanted your advice on something else. Another nondisclosure agreement, this time involving Mike Singer."

Her eyes narrowed. "Mike Singer? That's weird."

I took a swallow of coffee. "I know. There've been some financial improprieties involving a grant of Singer's, and I looked into his file to see if there had been any previous problems. Very strangely, there was no correspondence about his move here from Yale ten years ago, so I made a trip to New Haven to see if I could find out anything more about it."

She listened attentively as I told her about the payments to Sally Lipton, her refusal to talk to me, the nondisclosure agreement, and Martha Daniels's suicide. When I finished, she leaned her head back and shut her eyes. Then she said, "So you're thinking that his involvement with Lipton, which continues to present-day improprieties, was somehow tied into his being forced out of Yale?"

"There are plenty of other explanations, including innocuous ones. But yes, that's what I'm thinking. And I somehow need to figure out what's in that agreement."

"That's easier said than done. You're right that the Yale officials, including our current president, aren't going to talk to you about it. And it seems pretty clear that Sally Lipton isn't going to help either. That leaves Martha Daniels, who can't talk about anything anymore."

"I know. But I'd like to try to find out more about Martha Daniels. Maybe locate a friend she talked to about whatever happened at Yale."

Karen pursed her lips and nodded. "Yes, that might work. Maybe you'll make a detective someday after all. And just how are you going to find out more about Martha?"

"I was thinking of going up to Holderness and talking to people at the school. And to the cops who investigated her death. They would have interviewed her friends, wouldn't they?"

Karen smiled. "You're getting good. Yes, the cops would have talked to anyone close to her as part of investigating a suicide. But they aren't going to talk to you about it."

"I figured that. I was hoping—"

She laughed. "That I could help you out? Why not, I could use a little diversion. How about I pick you up at eight tomorrow morning, and we make a trip north to Holderness?"

———

The Holderness police department was a small building with white clapboard siding, right off Route 3 near Squam Lake, made famous as the location of the movie *On Golden Pond*. A nice place for a cop shop.

Karen showed her identification and asked if we could speak with the chief. The receptionist asked us to wait and went into an office with a placard reading CHIEF PATRICK ENGELS. After a minute, she beckoned us in, and Chief Engels got up from behind his desk to greet us. He was fiftyish, with close-cropped, gray hair and an expression that seemed to convey a permanent mixture of tolerance and mistrust.

"What's brought you folk all the way up here from Boston?" he asked.

"We're looking for information about a Martha Daniels." Karen handed him the newspaper obituary. "Suicide about eight years ago. We think she was involved in a case we're looking into concerning one of our faculty members."

He looked at the newspaper clipping. "Before my time, I'm afraid. Eight years ago, I was in Atlanta."

"Can we get a look at the case file, see who may have investigated it back then?" Karen asked.

"Sure." He handed the clipping to the receptionist. "Can you pull the file, please?"

She was back with the file in just a few minutes. An efficient operation.

Engels looked over the file first and then passed it to Karen and me. The police report was short but clear. Martha Daniels had been found hanging by a belt from her bedroom closet door frame. She'd left a brief note, printed out from her computer, apologizing to those she was leaving behind. An autopsy revealed some alcohol but no other drugs in her system. Several people interviewed had commented that she was unhappy with her position at the college and sometimes seemed seriously depressed. In the absence of any evidence to the contrary, suicide was the obvious conclusion.

When Karen and I looked up from the report, Engels said, "Seems pretty straightforward. Any help to you?"

"Not yet," Karen answered. "It's a bit thin. Are there any more details of the interviews with her friends? We'd like to find people who knew her."

"Sorry, that's all I've got," Engels said.

"How about the investigating officer?" Karen asked. "It's signed by a James O'Connell."

"The name's not even familiar," Engels said. "He must have left the force before I came on." He turned again to the receptionist. "Maybe Barb can find something in his personnel file for you."

We thanked Engels and followed Barb out to a file cabinet, from which she quickly pulled a new file. "James O'Connell retired six years ago. All we have is his phone number and address at that time." She wrote them on a piece of paper and handed it to Karen. "Good luck," she said.

———

Fortunately, James O'Connell kept the same phone number, which he answered on the fifth ring. He now lived in Moultonborough, about half an hour away. He was out fishing in what he called his backyard but said he would be happy to meet us at his house. And yes, he remembered the Martha Daniels case.

The house was small and more than a bit rundown, but it had the advantage of a secluded lot right on Lake Kanasatka. O'Connell greeted us when we pulled into the driveway and led us around the house to a large back deck overlooking the lake. There was a gas grill, a wooden dining table in the corner, and four Adirondack chairs with end tables arranged along the railing. If the house needed work, at least the deck was nicely outfitted.

He directed us to the Adirondacks, and I looked out at the lake. "So this is your backyard fishing hole? It's a great setting."

"I got it as a foreclosure. It needed some fixing up—still an ongoing project. But it's lakefront that a retired cop could afford, and I've got things in good shape back here. You guys want a beer or something?"

"It's beautiful," I said. "I'd love a spot like this. And a beer would be great."

Karen nodded her agreement, and O'Connell went in to fetch the beers. He returned with three bottles of Guinness and sat down. "So you're following up on Martha Daniels?"

I allowed myself to enjoy the view of the lake and have some beer while Karen answered. "She was involved in something that happened at Yale around ten years ago, and we were hoping to talk to her about it. Now we're looking for someone she may have talked to before she died. Did you interview any of her friends when you investigated her suicide?"

O'Connell nodded and picked up a folder next to him. "I pulled my old notes while you were coming over. The case was pretty clear cut, so it wasn't much of an investigation. I talked to three of her colleagues over at the college. They all said she was basically a loner, and they didn't know her well, but she seemed unhappy with her station in life. She also had a boyfriend, Bill Lawton, also a teacher at the college. He was pretty irrational about the whole thing—kept saying it was the fault of Yale University for ruining her life." O'Connell shrugged. "Crazy, but I guess he was trying not to feel guilty about her death."

"Why would he feel guilty?" I asked.

"They had a fight before she killed herself. But he said it wasn't any big thing. Happened every once in a while with her, and then they'd make up again."

"How well did this boyfriend know her?" Karen asked.

O'Connell consulted his notes. "Pretty well, I think. They'd been together a couple of years and talked of making it permanent, but according to him, she couldn't seem to commit herself. In fact, that's what he said they fought about."

"Sounds like we should talk to this boyfriend. Do you have contact info?"

He handed Karen a piece of paper. "Thought you might want to find him. He left town soon after her suicide, but this is his old phone and email. Maybe the college will have more."

Karen thanked him, and we got up to leave. Then she said, "One more thing. Did you ever find out more about what the boyfriend meant when he said it was Yale's fault?"

"Not really," O'Connell said. "The chief also interviewed him and thought he was a bit of a nut. Pot smoker and all, not worth listening to."

20

Once we got back to the car, I asked Karen what she was thinking.

"I don't know," she said. "It sounds like she was a depressed young woman who couldn't maintain a stable relationship and finally took her own life. But maybe it was all tied to something that happened back in New Haven. If it had been my case, I'd have kept working on that, whatever my boss thought about pot smokers."

"So we need to talk to the boyfriend?"

"Yes," she said. "I want to find out exactly what he meant about Yale being somehow responsible. And I want to find out more about Martha Daniels. Is there any chance she had any connections with Upton?"

"Christ. Not that I know of, but I suppose it's possible. Her research was in a similar field to his, and science can be a small world."

Karen pursed her lips. "Just thinking," she said. "Let's see if we can make contact with the boyfriend."

She took out the paper that O'Connell had given her and dialed a number on her phone. Then she shook her head and hung up. "No luck. It's been disconnected. I'll try sending an email asking him to call. Then let's go back to Holderness and stop in at the college where he and Martha worked. Maybe they'll have current contact info for him."

Karen's phone rang not long after we started back to Holderness. She grabbed it, listened for a minute, and pulled off the road. "Yes, this is Detective Karen Richmond. Thank you for calling back so promptly. My partner's here with me. Can I put you on speaker?"

I said, "Hello, this is Brad Parker." Karen had already identified me as her partner, so I figured I didn't need to give a fake police rank.

That was apparently right because the voice on the phone said, "Hello, this is Bill Lawton. Your email said you wanted to talk about Martha Daniels. She committed suicide several years ago. What can I do for you?"

"We're investigating a case in Boston that may be related to something that happened back when she was a student at Yale," Karen said. "We'd very much like to talk to you about her and anything she may have told you about her time there. But it would be much better to do this in person. Where are you located?"

"Those Yale years were bad for her. And the memory never left, no matter how much we loved each other." His voice cracked, and he paused for a minute. "Sure, I'll talk to you about her. I'm in Plymouth, New Hampshire. Where are you?"

"We're on the road heading from Moultonborough to Holderness."

"You're only half an hour or so away. Do you want to come now? I'll text you my address."

———

Lawton's address took us to a grungy-looking, two-story apartment complex with sparsely landscaped grounds, not far off the main road through Plymouth. We parked in an asphalt lot that was about half-full, went to the building entrance, and rang his apartment on an intercom in the lobby. Lawton buzzed us in and was waiting outside his door when we got to the second floor. He was tall and thin, dressed in jeans and a T-shirt with holes in it and *Patalonia College* on the front. His skin had an unhealthy gray tone, as if he seldom saw sunlight.

He led us into a small living room connected to a kitchen and dining area. It was clean but minimally furnished, with a TV across from a couch that looked like it had come from a cheap, secondhand outlet. He asked us to sit on the couch and grabbed one of the two wooden chairs from the kitchen table for himself. I was relieved that he didn't offer us anything to drink.

"Sorry," he said. "I know it's a bit cramped. But it's tough getting by on what I can scrape together these days as an adjunct. And I don't usually entertain. Mostly it's just me here."

"It's fine," Karen said. "Looks perfectly comfortable. So you aren't at Farmington anymore?"

"No, I couldn't stay after what happened to Martha. I quit and started drinking too much. And some other stuff." He looked at us warily. "Pot and some pills, I mean."

Karen nodded, and I shrugged. Our acceptance seemed to make him relax, and he continued. "Anyway, I went downhill for a while. Finally, I got into AA and pulled myself together enough to get a couple of adjunct teaching gigs. Then I moved here to make a fresh start." He gave us a wry half smile. "The idea of putting things behind me didn't work, of course, and I haven't been able to find another permanent position. But at least I earn enough as an adjunct at a few of the local schools to pay for food and rent."

I nodded sympathetically. "The adjunct business is tough."

We were quiet for a moment. Then Karen brought the conversation back on track. "We're so sorry about Martha. How long had the two of you been together?"

"Two years, more or less. We started seeing each other soon after she came to Farmington, and we really meshed. We were talking about living together, maybe even getting married, but she was never quite ready to take the leap."

"As I mentioned on the phone, we're particularly interested in something that she was involved in at Yale, before she came to Farmington. Did she ever talk about her time there?"

Lawton nodded. "Yes, something happened back then that left her bitter and angry. That's the main reason she wasn't ready to make things more permanent between us. She was unsettled—wasn't sure if she wanted the kind of life we had at Farmington or if she wanted to be at a big research university. When I asked her why she'd come to Farmington in the first place, she'd say that Yale had screwed her over."

"What'd she mean by that?" I asked.

"I don't know. She never wanted to talk about what happened. She'd just say stuff about damned big-shot faculty members doing whatever they wanted. Whatever it was, something back then derailed her career and left her bitter and angry. So much so that she couldn't even pursue a life together for us."

"I'm sorry," Karen said. "Did she ever say anything about what it was that hurt her? Or mention any names?"

"No names, but she'd sometimes go on a rant about how she could destroy their careers with her story. Bring some men at the top all the way down to the bottom of the pit. But that kind of anger would only come out if she had too much to drink or something. The next morning, she'd blow it off and say she couldn't talk about it."

We thanked him and started to leave. Then Karen said, "Sorry, but I need to ask you one more question. Do you think her anger about whatever happened back then contributed to her suicide?"

Lawton slumped back into his chair and put his head in his hands. "I'm sure it did. We had a fight that night, about getting married. As usual, she said she couldn't make a commitment until she knew what she was doing with her life, and those bastards at Yale had screwed her all up. She went home alone, and they found her the next morning."

He stood up again. "I can't talk about this anymore. I couldn't believe she committed suicide at first. Now I guess I've accepted it, although I still can't see why. I guess you can never really tell what's in another person's head. Even someone you love."

His eyes filled with tears as we left.

———

Karen pulled out of the parking lot.

"Not sure we learned much," I said. "Except something bad happened to her at Yale. Bad enough to drive her to her death."

"Yes," she said. "And whatever it was, it involved some powerful men. The way she kept quiet while being so bitter and angry smells of a nondisclosure agreement. Implying that Mike Singer was involved. We just don't know what happened or who else was part of it."

"Okay, I guess that's a bit more than we had. At least confirmation for what I already suspected. But what went on ten years ago in New Haven is still a blank."

"There must have been some connection between her and Singer. I think we have to look back there to find it."

"I already checked her publications. There's no connection to Singer. Or to Sally Lipton, for that matter."

"Yes, but publications would only reveal a major research tie, right? Maybe she took classes from Singer, or maybe he was on some faculty committee that evaluated her work. Something a little less direct than what you would have found."

I nodded. "You're right. There are lots of possible connections that I would have missed by just looking at published papers. What I need is her full academic record."

"Can you get it?"

"No, I can't access Yale's systems. But Martin Dawson can."

"The friend who got you into the record vault?"

"Yep. And this'll be a lot easier than that was. All he needs to do is pull her records from their graduate school files, which should be online." I pulled out my phone. "I'll email him now."

"Hold on," she said. "You probably both use university accounts, right?"

"Sure."

"Then don't use email. Just in case something gets weird, it'd be safer for BTI and Yale not to have access to your messages. Call or text him instead."

She was right. Martin and I had already pushed things with our illicit records gathering. I looked at my watch. "It's almost six now. I'll call him tomorrow."

"Sounds good," she said. "And if we're done detecting for the day, I think we deserve a little reward."

"What do you have in mind?"

"There's a country inn I know close by. Great place on the lake with a fabulous restaurant. Let's stay over and go back to Boston tomorrow morning."

I lit up with a thrill of anticipation. But a warning light started blinking in my head. "That sounds great. But I have to ask, what comes after? I'm sorry, but I don't think I can take any more roller-coaster rides."

She reached over and put her hand on my leg. "I know. No more roller coaster, I promise. I'm all in now."

I beamed at her as I felt her hand move to my growing erection. "Can you hold that thought for half an hour?" she asked.

"Drive fast," I said.

It only took twenty minutes to reach a side road with a carved wooden sign marking the turnoff for the Lakeside Inn. The wooded road led down to a large, colonial-style building with gray shingled walls accented by dark green shutters. We pulled the car into a guest parking area with a dozen or so spaces. Karen grabbed an overnight bag from the back seat, and we went inside to the registration desk.

"Reservation for Richmond," she said.

My jaw dropped, and I broke into a huge smile. "You planned this ahead?"

She squeezed my arm in response as the receptionist checked us in and directed us to a room on the second floor. It was furnished in traditional country style and featured a picture window with a striking view of Squam Lake.

"Beautiful," I said, looking out the window.

"Mmm, nice." I felt her snuggle in behind me, and I turned to take her in my arms. Our mouths met, and we kissed deeply before she led me to the canopied bed that dominated the room.

We made love twice, once fast and furious and the second time slow and tender. Then we dozed off for a bit. When I woke, she was lying in my arms, looking at me with a smile.

"About time you woke up. I'm starved."

I kissed her. "Want to get dressed and go down to the restaurant?"

She shook her head. "I'm good right here. Check out room service."

I called the restaurant. No room service, but they could bring something simple up. We settled for lobster rolls and a bottle of Sauvignon Blanc. Not a big hardship. We ate sitting in front of the window, wearing terrycloth robes we found in the bathroom. When we finished, Karen raised the bottom of her robe and moved onto my lap. "Time for dessert," she said.

This time we slept soundly afterward.

21

The clock on the bedside table said six when I opened my eyes. I hoped that meant we had time for a leisurely morning before heading back to Boston. But when I turned over and reached for Karen, the bed was empty. I was surprised by the wave of panic that came over me. *Had she left during the night?*

I sat up and called out—and felt an enormous sense of relief when she emerged from the bathroom. All of which must have shown in my face because she came over, sat next to me, and took my hand. "Don't worry," she said. "I'm not going anywhere."

I smiled sheepishly. "I'm sorry. I feel like an idiot. I was afraid you'd left."

"I understand. We've had more than our share of ups and downs. But I told you—I'm all in now."

I reached over to her, and she came into my arms. Our mouths met, but then she squeezed my shoulder and pulled away. "I'm afraid we do have to get home, though. I have a nine o'clock staff meeting, and it's one of those that I can't miss. How about picking this up tonight?"

———

Karen dropped me at my office, having made arrangements to meet at my place for dinner. All seemed well with the world, until I opened the door and was greeted by a whirring, grinding noise that made me think I'd gone to the dentist's by mistake. "Kristy," I yelled. "What the hell's going on?"

She turned off the source of the noise and looked up from the piles of paper on her desk. "Sorry, just shredding some sensitive stuff."

"Sounded like you were taking down the walls," I said. "What is it?"

"Good news for a change. Research accounting called yesterday to say they'd closed the audit. The auditors decided the consulting claims were appropriate, and they're giving us our money back."

"That's great. What was it all about?"

"I asked, but they said it was highly confidential. Just said to forget about it and destroy any related paperwork." She used her chin to point to the shredder. "So I'm being a good girl and enjoying the prospect of having our accounts balanced again."

I went through to my inner office and shut the door. It was nice that the auditors had resolved their problem, but why the insistence on secrecy? I'd never heard of orders to destroy files before. It was like someone was hiding something. And it only made me more curious. Even if the payments to Sally Lipton were legit, I still wanted to figure out what had gone on between her and Mike Singer back in New Haven. And what had happened to Martha Daniels.

I started by making the call to Martin Dawson that Karen and I had talked about yesterday. He answered on the second ring. "What's up, Parker? You must want something to be calling first thing in the morning. Or are you ready to come across with that dinner you owe me?"

I laughed. "Afraid you were right the first time. I need you to look up a former student's record for me. Martha Daniels, got her PhD in chemistry about ten years ago. Can you pull her transcript?"

"Sure, that's easy. Is this related to your interest in Mike Singer?"

"Yeah. Her name came up in his file, and I'd like to know more about her."

"What's the deal? What was in that file we hunted up anyway?"

I hesitated. Better not to tell him too much. "Sorry, but I really can't get into it on the phone. Could you just pull her file? I'll tell you all about it over the dinner I owe you. Maybe *dinners* after this."

"All right, all right. I'll download the file and email it to you."

"Not over university email. This isn't exactly legit, and I don't want there to be a traceable record in either of our accounts. Do you have a personal email, Gmail or something?"

"Sure. Want me to use that?"

"Please." I gave him my Gmail address.

"Okay, spymaster," he said. "I'll get it off to you shortly. You owe me big for this kind of cloak-and-dagger shit."

Martin's email came in a few hours later. Martha Daniels had no apparent involvement with Mike Singer—no classes or seminars with him, and he hadn't been on any of her thesis advisory committees. But she had taken a seminar course in her final year with Sally Lipton.

In the absence of any other connection, it looked like I'd have to take another go at Sally. Not a particularly pleasant prospect.

———

Dinner was Chinese takeout at my place. Karen had come prepared with a bottle of wine and, more importantly, a bag of treats from Polka Dog Bakery for Rosie. That won Rosie's heart, and she was sitting expectantly at Karen's feet as we unpacked an assortment of cardboard cartons on the dining table. Anyone who brought goodies from Polka Dog had to be a good prospect for a surreptitious treat at dinner.

Karen dipped a Peking ravioli in the ginger sauce. "Can she have some of this?"

"Sure, Chinese is her native food. But don't give her the sauce—it might be too spicy for her."

Karen tore off a sauce-free corner, which Rosie gratefully accepted. "They were bred as companions for Chinese royalty, weren't they? But they've evolved since then."

"Yes, they're an ancient Chinese breed. Professional lapdogs. How do you mean evolved?"

Karen grinned and gave Rosie another piece. "I'd say she's the royal one in this household, wouldn't you?"

I laughed. "Guess I can't argue with that. Anyway, how'd your day back at work go?"

"Lousy, to tell you the truth. The case is now officially cold. Everyone agrees on Upton, but he's left us nothing to go on."

I sighed. "Shit. What more can you do?"

"I wish I knew. To be honest, I'm afraid all we can do is hope that he somehow makes a mistake down the line and gives himself away. Sometimes killers like this will inadvertently say something to someone or play cat-and-mouse games with the cops. Without that, I'm afraid we're stuck. And he's already looking at a job at Berkeley."

I kept my lingering doubts about Upton to myself. No point getting into that argument tonight. Instead I served us some Kung Pao chicken. "Well, I had kind of an interesting day. I got into the office and found my administrator shredding all the files on our missing money. She'd been told that the auditors had resolved the problem with our accounts and to get rid of all her paperwork."

Karen raised an eyebrow. "What do you make of that? A rush to dispose of things always feels odd to me."

"Me too. Like someone has something to hide. Anyway, it reminded me to call my friend at Yale about Martha Daniels."

"And what'd your friend have to say?"

"He was happy to check out her transcript. No connection to Mike Singer, but she'd taken a seminar course taught by Sally Lipton."

Karen sipped her wine. "So an indirect link?"

"Maybe. I'm going to have to make another trip down to New Haven. Talk to Sally Lipton again and also look up Martha's thesis advisor. He'll at least know the story behind her going to the community college."

"That's a good idea, except I doubt if you'll get any further with Lipton than you did the first time."

"You're probably right. She seemed pretty determined not to talk to me. But what else can I do?"

"How about I go with you?"

"Why? You think she'll open up more to a woman?"

"I doubt it." Karen reached into her pocket and held up her badge. "But you'd be surprised how this gets people to talk."

22

Sally Lipton was in her office when we got there a little before eleven the next morning. She recognized me immediately. And didn't look happy about it.

"What do you want now? I already told you I don't have time to chitchat about Mike Singer."

I tried being nice. "I'm sorry to bother you again, but this'll just take a minute. We wanted to ask you about a former student, Martha Daniels."

"I don't know any Martha Daniels." She reached for the phone. "Get the hell out before I call security."

Karen held up her badge. "I'm Detective Karen Richmond. We just need a minute of your time."

The badge had the effect that Karen had predicted. Lipton scowled but put down the phone. "All right. What do you need to know?"

"Martha Daniels was a student in a course you taught ten years ago," Karen said. "Does that jog your memory?"

"A student from ten years ago?" She shrugged. "I've taught lots of students over the years. The name Martha Daniels doesn't ring a bell."

"The course was called Advanced Topics in Research," I said. "You still teach it, according to the course catalog. How many students are usually in it?"

Lipton rolled her eyes. "Just a dozen or so. It's an upper-level graduate course. Why do you care, for Christ's sake?"

I ignored her question. "Do you teach it yourself or with guest lecturers?"

"Damn it, I'm tired of this. What do you want from me? Get out of here!"

"Just answer the question." Karen's tone was harsh, accompanied by a cop interrogation look. "Unless you want us to make this more formal."

Lipton stared back at her. Then she said, "All right, fine. It's taught by multiple guest lecturers, each talking about the area of their research specialty."

"Do you have the roster from the year Martha Daniels took it?" I asked.

"From ten years ago? I doubt it."

Karen cleared her throat and ostentatiously looked around the office. "You seem to have an office full of filing cabinets. Well organized. I'm impressed. There's even one labeled *courses*. Think there might be a syllabus in there somewhere?"

Lipton turned red. "No, damn it. Leave me alone."

"Why don't you just take a look? Maybe you've forgotten. Unless you want us to come back with a warrant to search your office."

I knew it was a bluff, but Lipton didn't. "Screw you," she said. But she got up, went to the file cabinet, and threw half a dozen hanging folders in front of Karen.

"If I have anything, it'd be in here."

One of the folders was labeled *Advanced Seminar*. Karen leafed through it and came out with a syllabus for the year we wanted. She looked it over and passed it to me. There was a different guest lecturer each week of the course. Her finger was next to a name we both recognized.

Mike Singer.

Karen smiled and handed the folder back to Lipton. "Oh, this is great. Just what we wanted. Thanks so much for your cooperation."

Lipton stared at us as we got up and left her office.

I waited until we had walked down the hall to the elevators so that we wouldn't be overheard. Then I said, "So we have a connection. But it's pretty slim. Hard to see how Martha's being in a seminar course where Singer gave one or two lectures can amount to much."

Karen shrugged. "Who knows? Sometimes things add up in ways you don't expect. It's like that in your business too, no?"

"Yeah, I guess it is. More often than not, scientists just keep poking around until something opens up. Then maybe you have one of those rare bursts of clarity."

"So, let's go pay a visit to Martha's thesis advisor. Maybe he can add some clarity to the mix."

"Professor Clayton Marston," I said. "Sixth floor of this building. At least he's bound to be more fun than Sally Lipton."

I'd never met Marston, but I knew him well by reputation. Twenty-five years ago, when I was still a graduate student, he'd discovered a way to use fluorescence microscopy to study the movements of molecules in living cells. It was a discovery that revolutionized cell biology and earned him a host of major accolades, including one of Yale's coveted endowed professorships and membership in the National Academy of Sciences.

I didn't know what to expect when we knocked on his door, but being politely greeted by a short, slightly plump man with long white hair and a pleasant smile wasn't it. He directed us to seats on a couch in the corner of his office, which was large enough to fit his stature as a major scientific force. The walls seemed to be decorated equally with awards from a variety of learned societies and with family pictures that looked like they spanned at least three generations.

He saw me looking around his office and said, "Yes, I've been blessed with quite a crop of children and grandchildren. Two sons and a daughter, all with families of their own now."

"And there's been significant recognition of your many scientific accomplishments too," I said.

He smiled and shrugged. "I suppose. At my age, the family stuff seems more important. Anyway, what can I do for you?"

"We'd like to ask about one of your former students," I said. "Do you remember a Martha Daniels? She got her degree, with you as her thesis advisor, about ten years ago."

The smile faded when I said her name. "Of course, I remember all my students. When I look back over my career, it's my students who are most important to me. Many are doing quite well at universities and research institutions all around the world, and I love to follow their accomplishments. But not Martha. She was one of my failures."

His face tightened, and he looked down at the floor. "She was bright, ambitious, and hardworking. Wonderful in the lab, maybe one of the best students I ever had. She had an illustrious future ahead of her, and suddenly it all went wrong."

"I'm so sorry," Karen said. "What happened?"

"I wish I knew. It was her last year before finishing her degree. She had a junior faculty fellowship at Harvard all lined up and was excited about getting her papers out and moving on with her career. And it would have been a special one."

He shook his head and stopped talking. "What went wrong?" I prompted.

His eyes were moist. "I'm sorry—I feel so badly about this. I don't really know what happened. All of a sudden, she just changed. It was like she became a different person, bitter and angry. She turned down the job at Harvard and took a teaching position at a small community college in New Hampshire. I couldn't get her to talk about it or explain her change of heart. All she'd say is that something had happened that showed her what getting ahead in science really took. And it wasn't for her. Then two years later, she killed herself."

I could feel his pain. But there was more that we needed to know. "And you don't have any idea what she was talking about? It must have been a major trauma," I said.

"Obviously, but she'd never say what it was. I tried to talk to her many times, but she'd just clam up and say she'd made her decision."

He looked so forlorn that Karen reached over and squeezed his hand. "I'm sure you did all you could to help her," she said. "Did she have a boyfriend? Anyone she was close to and might have talked to about this?"

His voice was shaky now. "I don't think there was a serious boyfriend. Occasionally she'd bring a date to lab parties, but never the same young man more than once or twice. But she was close to another student in the lab, Linda Chen. They were roommates the whole time they were here. I think if Martha opened up to anyone, it would have been Linda."

"Do you know how we can get in touch with Linda?" I asked.

"She went from here to a faculty appointment at Princeton, but she didn't get tenure there and had to leave. I believe she's someplace in the Midwest now, maybe Michigan or Wisconsin. Some big school like that."

"Thank you," I said. "We appreciate your help. And it's been an honor to meet you."

We left him alone with his thoughts. He didn't get up or say goodbye.

———

Karen took the wheel for the drive back so that I could search for Linda Chen. PubMed made it easy. She published frequently and in top journals. Hard to see why she hadn't made tenure at Princeton. At least from her publication record, she'd have been a shoo-in at BTI. Probably being a woman hadn't helped. Anyway, she was now a tenured professor in the Department of Chemistry at the University of Wisconsin–Madison, a top-ranked department. She'd done well after leaving Princeton. I went to her website and saw that she directed a large research group of a dozen or so graduate students and research fellows. And that she was teaching this semester. Meaning that she'd be on campus, and I could pay her a visit.

"Want to make a trip to Madison to visit Linda Chen tomorrow?" I asked Karen.

"Sorry, I'm going to have to get back to work. You can handle this one on your own, right?"

"It's more fun with you, but sure."

I started to check on flights to Madison but was interrupted by my phone's ringtone. I did a double take when I saw the call was from the BTI Office of the President. The voice on the other end of the line identified himself as the president's executive assistant, Doug Westman.

"President Emerson would like to see you tomorrow morning, ten o'clock," he said.

I'd never been asked to see the president before, except as part of large group meetings that were ceremonial in nature. If that's all this was, I could send a substitute and go ahead to Madison. "May I ask what the meeting's about? I'm planning to be out of town tomorrow, and perhaps I could ask someone else from the department to take my place."

"No, Professor Parker. The president needs to see *you*. He'll explain when you're here. Please cancel whatever else you have scheduled. We'll see you tomorrow morning."

23

The Central Administration Building, otherwise known as the Presidential Palace, was an imposing ten-story structure with a gleaming granite and glass facade; marble floors; and a striking, all-white interior. I arrived ten minutes late, a gesture intended to express my resentment at the peremptory summons that brought me here. On the other hand, I wore my one and only suit, purchased two years ago for my son's wedding. I wasn't sure what kind of mixed message I was trying to send. Maybe that I was some sort of independent conformist.

The receptionist on the top floor seemed unfazed by either my tardiness or my attire. She said the president would be with me shortly and directed me to a waiting area next to a floor-to-ceiling window with a breathtaking view of the Charles River. I took a seat on an overstuffed couch and started leafing through one of the copies of the BTI alumni magazine that were spread out on a side table. Several copies of President Emerson's recently published memoir, *The Academic Life*, were also there, waiting to be perused.

They kept me waiting ten minutes, just long enough to establish that my time was less valuable than Emerson's, before the receptionist took me into his office. It was big enough to house at least two laboratories. Two of the walls were dark wood paneling, covered with oil paintings in gold frames. Fine art wasn't my area of expertise, but they looked like they belonged in a museum. The other two walls were glass, one with the view of the Charles River I'd had in the waiting area and the other with a cityscape of downtown Boston. Several conference tables and seating areas of different sizes were scattered around the room, and the floor was covered with two oversize Chinese rugs.

Emerson got up from his desk to greet me, and we met halfway across the office.

"Thank you for coming to see me," he said. "I'm a great admirer of the work you've done with our Integrated Life Sciences Department. It's become a real center of excellence in the institute. The rape and murder of your poor student sullied things, of course, but I understand you even handled that as well as anyone could have."

He sounded like I was here for a friendly chat. Not like I'd been dragged in for a command performance. I thanked him and waited for what was to come next.

"Would you care for some tea? I always find it helps me relax, and I've had a hard morning already," he said. "An eight o'clock fundraiser with members of the board of directors."

"I'm fine, thank you," I said.

"No, please join me." He walked over to a granite counter near his desk. "Do you like Earl Grey? Or I can offer green tea, if you prefer."

"Whatever you're having, thank you."

"Good, Earl Grey it is, then." He poured bottled water into an electric tea kettle and spooned the tea into tea balls. When the water was ready, he served the tea in mugs with gold BTI insignias. I declined milk or lemon, and he led us to a seating area with leather armchairs and a marble coffee table. I had the view of downtown and was pretty sure I could see the roof of my condo building.

He took a sip of his tea and smiled. "So good of you to come talk with me. I seldom have a chance to meet with real scientists anymore. Most of my time seems to be spent raising money, protecting the institution from damaging legislation, things like that. And of course, dealing with all manner of problems that threaten to derail our mission. That's why I so admire the good work you've done in your department. Wonderful to see."

"Thank you. I appreciate the kind words."

"Doing the administrative work is hard, isn't it? I mean, you're an accomplished scientist, and now you've also had to deal with some of the same kind of administrative problems I face in this office."

"Only on a much smaller and simpler scale," I said. Where was this going?

"Not always so simple, is it? We always have to be careful to make sure we're supporting our most productive faculty, don't we? That's where the real strength of either a department or the entire institution lies."

I drank some tea. "Most definitely. Although I think it's also important to be fair with everyone and to give our young faculty every opportunity to develop their careers. After all, that's where the future lies."

"Yes," he said, "but it's the top senior faculty who determine a department's standing. Who would you say is your best faculty member?"

I hesitated. This wasn't a game I wanted to play with the president of the institute. "Well, we have several outstanding people. I don't think I could name just one."

He put down his mug and frowned at me. "Come now, that's ridiculous. Surely you know who your top faculty member is. Michael Singer."

"Well, he's certainly up there."

"Up there indeed! He's by far your best in terms of grants, papers, awards—however you want to measure it. And if you're going to lead your department effectively, that's not something you should ignore." The old boys' friendliness was gone now, replaced by the demeanor of an annoyed senior executive talking to a subordinate who doesn't quite get it.

"Of course not," I said.

"Then perhaps you can explain why you've been poking around Yale, asking questions about Mike's ancient history?"

I drank some more tea to stall for time. So this was why we were here. Maybe he was embarrassed by his signature on Singer's nondisclosure agreement. But how did he know about my visits to New Haven?

"The accounting office was investigating some irregularities involving consulting payments to a Yale faculty member from Singer's grants. I made a trip down there to talk to her about it, hoping I could clear things up."

"Sally Lipton. Yes, she complained about your visits. Apparently, you barged into her office twice, the last time accompanied by one of our institute detectives." He leaned forward and furrowed his brow. "That is totally inappropriate. It's not your business to act as an investigator and certainly not to involve the institute police in your inquiries. Your job is to support your faculty."

"As I said, I was hoping that Dr. Lipton could clear things up."

"Then it seems particularly odd for you to have made your second visit *after* the auditors concluded that the consulting payments were appropriate and terminated the inquiry. And I understand you were also asking about a former student, Martha Daniels. What does she have to do with it?"

Lipton's complaints weren't a big surprise—but to the president of BTI? What the hell was going on?

Emerson got up and raised his voice an octave. "Never mind. Don't bother trying to answer. But listen carefully. I want you to stop screwing around with this. Just back off and treat Singer like the outstanding scientist that he is. If I hear of any more inquiries, I'll have your job."

I stood up too. Something was really weird for him to get involved like this. "You can have my resignation as department chair anytime you want. I'll happily go back to being an ordinary faculty member. I'd love to be able to focus on my research."

"You think being a tenured professor will protect you? You're a fool. It'd take a bit of effort, but I can easily enough get a revocation of your tenure too. Just keep looking into Singer if you want to see me do it."

———

I headed over to the river when I left the Presidential Palace. The meeting had been bizarre, and I needed to try to make some sense of it. Whatever Emerson was afraid that I might find out had to be big. Big enough to make him cross the ultimate academic line of threatening to fire a tenured faculty member. And despite the nonchalance of his threat, he wouldn't be able to pull that off without a formal academic proceeding that would take months of work by several faculty committees. Getting rid of tenured faculty members was a big deal that would generate a ton of publicity and probably result in intervention by organizations that were dedicated to protecting academic freedom. The American Association of University Professors and the like. It just wasn't something that a university president would want to do.

So what was this about? He clearly hoped and expected that his combination of cajoling and bullying would make me drop the matter. Perhaps he'd offered Singer such a sweet retention deal at Yale that he didn't want word to get out. Maybe there was some kind of relationship between them that would be a substantial embarrassment for the current president of BTI. That would explain the nondisclosure agreement as well as his going so far as to threaten me.

Possible, but if that was it, Sally Lipton and Martha Daniels would presumably have to know what it was all about for them to have signed the agreement. And they were both awfully far down the totem pole of academic life to be included in details of a senior faculty retention.

So that left the possibility that Singer had been forced to leave Yale because of some type of misconduct—something nasty that was covered by the agreement and that Emerson didn't want to become public. Like the illicit use of research funds, which was why I'd started looking into this in the first place. Some kind of sustained scam with Sally Lipton that had started in New Haven and continued to the present day. A fraud that Emerson would most certainly want to cover up if he'd offered Singer an easy way out at Yale and then continued to support his career at BTI.

I didn't like being bullied, and Emerson's involvement had the opposite effect from what he wanted. Somehow or other, I was going to find out what had happened at Yale ten years ago that was so important.

I checked my watch. Not quite eleven. Plenty of time to catch an early afternoon flight to Madison.

Maybe Linda Chen was the key.

24

The Department of Chemistry's website told me that Linda Chen taught an organic chemistry class from ten to eleven the next morning, so I figured the best way to catch her would be to show up right after her lecture. I got to the lecture hall at about ten forty-five and slipped into a seat in the back. As I expected, it was a big class. Maybe two hundred students. To her credit, almost all of them seemed to be paying attention. In fact, I'd give her high marks as a lecturer if I were here to evaluate her teaching. She was animated and kept the class engaged by asking questions and throwing in colorful anecdotes and the occasional joke as she went along.

When she concluded, half a dozen students went up to the front of the room with their books or lecture notes open. I waited at the back of the group while she answered their questions. When she finished, she turned to me with a smile. "Hi, I'm Linda Chen. Are you here evaluating my teaching for the Weinstein Award?"

I returned the smile. "No, but I'd give you high marks if I was. You're an impressive lecturer."

She looked puzzled. "Then who are you?"

"Brad Parker. I'm chair of the Integrated Life Sciences Department at the Boston Technological Institute. I'm hoping I can get a few minutes of your time to ask you about someone you knew when you were a graduate student at Yale. Martha Daniels."

"I'm sorry—I don't think I can help you. I don't remember anyone by that name." She started to walk away.

"Wait, please," I said. "Clayton Marston said the two of you were roommates when you both worked in his lab as graduate students. I wouldn't have come all this way if it wasn't important."

She closed her eyes and shook her head. "All right. Let's go find a place where we can talk."

"Your office?" I suggested.

"No, the Memorial Union is right next door. We can get a cup of coffee and sit by the lake."

We got coffees and took them out to the terrace, overlooking the expanse of Lake Mendota. It was a chilly November day, maybe just hitting fifty degrees, but the terrace was crowded with students and faculty enjoying the view.

Linda maneuvered us to a table at the fringes of the crowd. It was a place we could talk privately but where we wouldn't be alone. I wondered if that's what she had in mind when she suggested it. Or maybe she just liked having coffee here.

"You're right," she said. "Martha and I were close friends as well as roommates. But why are you interested in her now? It's been several years since her death."

"I've been looking into a case of possible misconduct involving one of the faculty members in my department at BTI. It led me back to Yale, and Martha's name came up. I understand that she underwent a big change in her professional direction right at the end of her graduate student career, and it may be important for me to find out what happened. Professor Marston thought that if anyone knew, it would be you."

She looked out at the lake. "Yes, something happened all right. Everybody who knew Martha could tell that. But she made me promise never to speak of it. Warned me not to, really."

"Warned you?"

"She said talking about it would only bring me trouble. That there were powerful men involved." She sat up straight in her chair and furrowed her brow. "And now, ten years later, you're asking about it. How do I even know you're who you say you are? This could be some kind of sick test, for all I know."

I gave her my BTI photo ID card, and she examined it briefly.

"Okay, so you're Brad Parker," she said. "BTI is where that girl was raped and murdered recently, isn't it? Did you know her?"

A wave of sadness hit me as it came back. "Yes, I knew her. She was a student in my department."

Linda gasped. "Oh my God, I'm so sorry! That must be horrible for you."

I tried to drink some coffee, but my hands were shaking. At least she seemed to have accepted me now. "What can I say? It's awful to have that happen to someone you know."

"I'm sorry," she said again. "I read about it, of course. It was all over the news." Then her eyes widened. "Wait, that's not why you're asking me about Martha, is it?"

"No, it's a different case that led me to Martha. A financial problem. Why do you ask that?"

Linda Chen took a deep breath. "Because Martha was raped. That's what I was never, ever supposed to tell anyone."

My mouth opened as the shock wave hit me. So Singer hadn't been involved with financial shenanigans at Yale—but with a rape case! And if he was accused of rape back then, could it be him now? Except his alibi was solid.

Linda didn't notice my surprise and stared out at the lake as she continued. "She went to a party given by one of her course instructors and didn't come back until the next morning. A total mess, and she couldn't even remember much. She said one of the faculty members who was there took her to a back bedroom, and she passed out, but she remembered him assaulting her."

"Did she say anything about what happened?"

Linda fidgeted in her chair and spoke in a soft voice, as if she was still embarrassed for her friend. "He pulled down her jeans and stuck his fingers in her. She thought he must have put something in her drink to knock her out."

"What a bastard! Did she know who it was? I hope she brought charges."

"She knew, and she immediately went to the dean's office to file a complaint. But the faculty member denied it, and it was just her word against his. They said that she didn't have any proof, and they couldn't allow her to slander an innocent faculty member. Then the dean threatened to expel her from school if she didn't sign some kind of agreement to keep the whole thing confidential."

I sighed. "That's disgusting. I'd like to think it wouldn't happen that way now, but who knows. Who was the faculty member?"

"Martha wouldn't tell me. She was afraid of what might happen if word got out that she talked. All she would say was that he was a big shot, and that's why she got screwed. In the end, she was so disgusted with the way the whole system turned on her that she left science. And eventually killed herself. She sent me an email before she did it, saying that those scumbags at Yale had ruined her life. She couldn't go on anymore after what they did to her."

"She sent you a suicide note? And you didn't get it in time to stop her? My God, that must have been horrible for you."

"She used delay send, so I didn't get it until hours after she was dead. There was nothing I could do."

Linda swallowed the rest of her coffee in one large gulp. There were tears in her eyes as she got up to go.

"Wait, there's one more thing," I said. "Did you know a faculty member by the name of Sally Lipton?"

"I took a course from her, I think the year before Martha was raped. It was one of those advanced seminar courses where a whole bunch of different faculty members come in to give lectures on their research areas. And she always had a party for the students and faculty in the middle of the semester so they could get to know each other informally. It was kind of nice. Except not for Martha. It was at one of Lipton's parties that she was attacked."

I played with the rest of my coffee as Linda left, extracting one more promise that I wouldn't tell anyone that she'd talked to me.

She didn't know who Martha Daniels's rapist was, but I was pretty sure I did.

Mike Singer.

And maybe I was beginning to see how he'd fooled us.

25

My mind was still swirling as I took an aisle seat on the six-thirty flight home from Madison. I could put a story together at this point, all pointing at Mike Singer. It seemed pretty clear that he'd assaulted Martha Daniels years ago in New Haven. It had happened at one of Sally Lipton's parties, and I was willing to bet that she'd seen something, which would explain her name on the nondisclosure agreement. And the dean responsible for shutting down Martha's complaint had been Kenneth Emerson. The current president of BTI. The same asshole who'd tried to shut me down yesterday.

I was pretty confident about what had happened at Yale. And if Mike Singer was a rapist ten years ago, why not now? The implication that he was the one who'd assaulted Emily was unavoidable. An assault that involved drugging and then manually penetrating the victim, just like the attack on Martha Daniels.

The only problem was his alibi, which placed him firmly in his office when Emily was assaulted. But what Linda had told me about the suicide note she received from Martha Daniels might hold the key to that too. I googled "delay send email." The lead entry was clear.

Delay the delivery of a single message.

It described how to schedule an email to be sent automatically at any desired time after it was written. Martha Daniels used it to send her suicide note to Linda after she was dead. And Mike Singer could have used it to fake what had seemed like a convincing alibi.

So was Mike Singer, my colleague and an eminent scientist, really a rapist and a murderer? And just how much was Emerson trying to protect him from?

I needed a reality check. A talk with Karen to see what a professional would say. I texted her that I'd be home around eleven and had quite a story to tell. Her response was immediate.

I've got some news to talk about too. Meet you at your place.

I was trying to puzzle that out when a tap on my shoulder broke my concentration. "Excuse me, could I get by for a minute? I'm in the window seat."

I looked up at a red-haired woman in a gray wool skirt and black suit jacket standing in the aisle.

"Of course." I got up and moved into the aisle while she maneuvered across the row to take her seat. She looked vaguely familiar, but I couldn't quite place her. "I feel like we've met," I said. "Do I know you from somewhere?"

She looked at me coldly. Maybe she thought I was trying for a quick pickup. "I don't think so," she said. "Anyway, I have work to do."

She focused her attention on her laptop, effectively demonstrating that she had no interest in chatting. Which was fine—I had enough to think about.

Maybe I was letting my imagination run away with me. Just because Singer had been involved in a sexual assault ten years ago in New Haven, it didn't mean that he'd become a serial rapist and murderer. And Emerson might have used the nondisclosure agreement as the best way to get rid of him. Nothing sinister, just like our dean had gotten rid of Steve Upton. And with all the money Singer was bringing in for the institute, an amount that could soar with the licensing of Immunoboost, it wasn't surprising that Emerson wanted to prevent further scandal by my raising a nasty incident that was now far in the past. Sure, the assaults on Emily and Martha were similar. Drugged and then raped. But that was a common-enough scenario that it didn't necessarily mean the same person was responsible. Wasn't Upton still the obvious candidate?

My mental ping-pong was interrupted when my seatmate muttered an apology and squeezed across me to the aisle. She didn't give me a chance to get up and let her out but was in such a hurry that she crawled over me, muttering a startled "Oh!" when the back of one of her legs rubbed against me. Then she turned and glared at me before going over to the flight attendant who was serving drinks a few rows behind us. They spoke briefly, and the attendant escorted her to another seat at the front of the plane. Then he came back to pick up my former seatmate's laptop and bag from the overhead compartment.

"Is there a problem?" I asked.

He looked at me blankly. "No, she just needed to move her seat."

"Oh, did she know somebody up there?"

He shrugged. "Maybe. It's not your concern, okay?"

Weird, I thought. As if I'd somehow offended her, but we hadn't even spoken since she sat down. Maybe I was supposed to be telepathic and know when she wanted to get out of her seat without her needing to say anything. Something else to ponder. A little break from thinking about Mike Singer.

———

I got off the plane eager to get home and see Karen when four of them converged on me. Two state troopers in uniform and two guys in conservative dark suits.

The uniforms blocked my path, and one of the suits asked, "Are you Professor Brad Parker?"

"Yes. Is there a problem?"

"We need you to come with us."

What the hell was this? "Wait a minute. What's going on?"

He flashed a badge. "I'm Special Agent Larson, FBI. Again, we need you to come with us. Now."

"Look, I need to get home. Just tell me what this is all about."

"Fine, we'll do it the hard way." He turned to one of the uniforms. "Cuff him."

One of the troopers grabbed my arms behind me and slapped handcuffs on. I started to struggle but got hold of myself. Resisting would only make things worse, whatever was going on.

"All right," I said. "Wait a minute—you don't need those."

"Screw it. Just bring him," Larson ordered.

They marched me through the airport, a perp walk with my hands cuffed behind me. We went down to the lower level, and they led me to a room in the bowels of the airport, behind the baggage claim area, away from normal passenger traffic. It was small and windowless, with no carpeting and painted a dull institutional gray with a single fluorescent light in the ceiling. The only furniture was a stark metal table with several chairs scattered around. A video camera was mounted on the wall.

"If you sit down and stop being an asshole, I'll let him take the cuffs off," Larson said.

I glared at him but took a chair. The uniform uncuffed me, and Larson sat at the table across from me.

"So will you tell me what this is all about now?" I asked.

He held up his phone and showed me a picture. "Do you know this woman?"

It was the woman who'd been seated next to me on the flight. "Not really. She was sitting next to me on the plane, but I don't know who she is."

He stood up and leaned over in my face. "You don't, huh? She's the woman you assaulted when she tried to get out of her seat to go to the bathroom. You stuck your hand up her skirt and grabbed her ass. Do you remember that, you damned pervert?"

"Wait a minute! Nothing like that happened!"

"Oh no? Did she keep her seat next to you for the whole flight?"

"No. She got up and said something to the flight attendant. He moved her to a new seat."

"And you're telling me you don't know why? You're unbelievable." He was shouting now.

I tried to stay calm. "No, I don't know why she wanted to move. I never touched her."

"You're a liar. She told the flight attendant what you'd done, so he moved her and called us to meet the plane. Two other passengers confirmed her story."

"No, that's just not true." This was the kind of situation where I knew that anything I said would be disbelieved. But I couldn't keep myself from trying. "Absolutely nothing like that happened. This is ridiculous."

"Ridiculous, is it? Are you aware that sexual assault on an airplane is a federal crime? That's why you're talking to the FBI, asshole. And I don't think you'll find federal prison to be ridiculous. Not a pansy college professor like you."

I took a deep breath and tried to fight the panic rising in me. "Look, all I can say is that I didn't assault her. And I want to talk to a lawyer."

"That's the first smart thing you've said so far." He picked up his file. "And apparently someone's looking out for you. I understand your legal beagle is already on his way."

He turned and left, slamming the door behind him. I got up and tried it, even though I knew it'd be locked. It was. I sat back down to wait.

Where was a lawyer coming from? Karen could have sent one, but how did she know about my predicament? And more than that, what the hell was going on?

Time passed slowly. I had my phone, so I tried texting Karen. But no service—they presumably had the room blocked. I was sure the cops were watching, but I restrained myself from yelling at the video camera. Better to stay in control and wait for the unknown lawyer to appear.

It was almost three hours later when there was a knock on the door and two suits came in. The first, a tall, slim guy with silver hair, introduced himself as being from the BTI Office of General Counsel. His companion was Doug Westman, executive assistant to the president.

Westman took the lead. "You'll recall that we spoke by phone two days ago to arrange the meeting you had with President

Emerson yesterday?" He stared at me with unblinking gray eyes that looked as cold as he'd sounded on the phone.

"I remember," I said. "But how did you know I was here?"

He ignored the question. "It seems like you didn't understand what President Emerson said to you. He told you to stay the hell away from Mike Singer, didn't he?"

I returned the cold stare. "What's that have to do with anything?" I turned to the lawyer. "Who called you guys to come down here? And more important, how about getting me out of this mess?"

"Who called us doesn't matter," Westman said. "What does matter is that you don't seem to have gotten President Emerson's message. You went straight from his office to Madison, sticking your nose in the wrong place again."

So somehow this was all tied in with Mike Singer. But how did they know what I'd done after meeting with Emerson? And were they really using these charges to get me to back off?

"I don't see what that has to do with these ridiculous allegations," I said.

Westman handed me a letter. "Ah yes, the allegations. Unfortunately, we don't think they're ridiculous at all." He sniffed. "Quite credible, actually. This is formal notice of your removal from the position of department chair and your placement on administrative leave from your faculty appointment. You are to stay away from campus and avoid any contact with students until the matter is resolved. And I would suggest that you follow President Emerson's advice about terminating your illicit investigative activities."

"There are two ways this can play out," the lawyer said. "It could be that your seatmate will decide not to press charges, and the whole matter will be dropped. Unfortunately, if she decides to go ahead, it looks like the case against you is quite strong. What you've done is a federal offense, and I can tell you that they come down hard on this kind of thing. You could be looking at years in prison. Not something you want to mess around with."

"You could help yourself by voluntarily leaving BTI," Westman said. "We'd ask you to resign and sign a nondisclosure agreement covering any information you have pertaining to Mike Singer. In that case, I'm sure we could get the charges dropped. You'd be free to find another position and move on with your life."

I looked from one to the other. So they were using this to shut me up and get rid of me. Just as Emerson had threatened. But I'd never imagined an academic playing this kind of hardball.

I clenched my fists and forced myself to stay cool. Or at least try to appear cool. "I'll need a little time to consider," I said. "In the meantime, can you get me out of here?"

The lawyer nodded. "Yes, I've made the necessary arrangements for your release. You're free to go for now."

"Think carefully about your next move," Westman said. "I'll need to hear from you within the next two days or our offer is off the table. And I don't think you want to know what will happen after that."

My teeth were clenched as I watched them go down the hall and out of sight. Then I followed them out of the room. The airport was dark and deserted at this hour of the morning, giving it a ghostlike appearance. My heart was going a mile a minute, and all I really wanted to do was to smash Westman's face to a bloody pulp. Then I thought of Karen. It was almost two in the morning—I couldn't imagine what she must be thinking.

I grabbed my phone, which now had a signal again. And was surprised to find a text from Karen waiting for me.

I found out what's happened. I'm so sorry! Somehow you must have been set up. Try to get some rest. I'll be over in the morning. Rosie's all taken care of. Don't worry, we'll figure this out. Xoxo

I reread the message and gave a sigh of relief. At least Karen believed in me. She'd probably be the only one. This was the kind of offense where everyone automatically assumed the accused was guilty. As had happened to Steve Upton.

And it didn't leave me many options, other than accepting their offer and getting out of BTI under a protective cloak of silence.

26

The last thing I remembered was getting home and sinking into a chair with a big glass of scotch and Rosie on my lap. I guess I made my way to bed at some point after that because I woke up to find Karen snuggled beside me. She must have felt me stir because she rolled over and put her arms around me. Then she kissed me, exploring my mouth with her tongue. A nice way to get my mind off my problems. Then she moved her head down my chest, my stomach, and between my legs. I stopped thinking.

The smell of coffee greeted me when I woke a second time. Ten o'clock. I got out of bed to find Karen in the kitchen.

"Glad you caught some sleep," she said. "I take it you don't have to be at work?"

"No. Among other things, they put me on leave and banned me from campus. But how about you?"

She gave a disgusted snort. "Pretty much the same story. They appointed my old boss as the new chief. You know, the bastard I told you about from Boston PD. He gave me a month to find a new job." She shrugged. "I have more than that in unused vacation time, so no pressure on me to go in. They don't want me around anyway."

"Shit, I'm sorry. That son of a bitch."

"Don't worry about it. It's nothing like what happened to you. There are plenty of other universities. The whole country's full of them. I'll find something. I already heard from a friend in Chicago offering me something out there."

I swallowed hard. A new threat to our relationship, on top of everything else. I wasn't sure I could take any more. "In Chicago? Are you considering it?"

The expression on my face must have portrayed my feelings. She came over and gave me a hug. "Let's not sweat that for now. We'll figure things out. First we need to take care of you."

It wasn't quite what I wanted to hear, but I could tell that I wasn't going get anything more at the moment. So I poured some coffee and took a croissant from a box she had open on the counter. "Where'd these come from?"

"I stopped at the Bread Place on my way over." She hesitated and then passed a copy of the newspaper over to me. "I'm afraid they had this too."

I was on the front page of the *Boston Globe*, picture and all. *Professor arrested for sexual assault on airline.* The article took pains to point out that BTI had responded quickly and forcefully: I'd been removed from my position as department chair and put on leave, barred from any contact with students.

The bile rose in my throat, and I had to sit down. This was it. They'd gone public. My only chance was to accept their shit offer and get the charges dropped. Even then, I'd have to get out of Boston if I was to have any chance of finding another job in academia.

"We've got to figure out what happened," Karen said. "I know the basics and that the institute lawyer got you out. But fill in the details for me."

I took a while to go through the events of the past two days, starting with my meeting with President Emerson.

Karen listened intently without interrupting. Then she said, "They set you up."

"By *they*, you mean the institute? I thought of that, too, of course. But how could they even know I went to Wisconsin? Let alone pull off something like this."

"I'll bet they had you followed as soon as you left Emerson's office."

My jaw dropped. "You've got to be kidding! This isn't the CIA. They don't do crap like that."

She raised her eyebrows. "Oh no? I'm afraid you've got a lot to learn about how big institutions work. Why do you think universities have their own police forces?"

I didn't try to answer that one. Instead I took a bite of the croissant. "All right, I guess you should know."

She nodded. "Think about the woman on the plane. Had you ever seen her before?"

"I thought she looked vaguely familiar when she sat next to me. But I can't think from where."

"Close your eyes and picture her face, her hair, her clothing, whatever you can remember. It's important. Now try to place where you've seen her. At Emerson's office? Maybe on the flight you took out to Wisconsin?"

"No, I don't think so," I said. Then it came to me. Red hair and a black jacket. "Wait, she was at the outdoor café. The student union where we had coffee. Sitting a few tables away from us. I noticed that she looked out of place in a skirt and business jacket. Everyone else was dressed informally, like students or faculty members usually are."

Karen nodded and pursed her lips. "Hang on a minute." She grabbed her phone and scrolled through it. Then she showed me the screen. "Any of these women look familiar?"

There were photos of five women. My jaw dropped when I looked at the third. It was the woman from the plane. "How the hell did you do that? That's her!"

"They're pictures of my colleagues. Meet the female BTI cops. Your little friend here is Ann Collins, assigned for special duty in the president's office. She must have followed you out to Madison, tailed you there, and then set you up on the flight back."

I was starting to catch on. "So she knew who I talked to in Madison. And then presumably reported back here."

Karen nodded. "And then got instructions to fake an assault and get you arrested when the plane landed."

"But how could she have managed to sit next to me? Just dumb luck?"

"There are advantages to being a cop. All she had to do was tell the ticket agent that she was following you and wanted an adjacent seat."

I stood up and went over to the window. People were walking outside with their dogs as if it were a perfectly normal day. Unknowing.

"So what do I do? They've boxed me into an impossible position." I picked up the newspaper. "Especially now that it's public."

"I think you tell them that you'll accept their deal," she said.

I smiled sadly. "That sounds good, doesn't it? We could both look for jobs away from Boston—Chicago or wherever. Start over together. But I can't do it. If I'm right, Singer is a rapist and a murderer. Being protected by the president of BTI."

She gave a mock sigh. "Sometimes you don't listen carefully. I didn't say you should accept their deal, not for real. I said you should *tell them* you're going to accept it. Buy yourself a little time."

I went over and kissed her forehead. "Thanks, I'm glad you don't want me to fold and just walk away. But still, what can we do?"

"First, let's back up for a minute. What you've learned tells us that Singer was guilty of sexual assault ten years ago in New Haven and that our current institute president was involved in sweeping it under the rug. Bad stuff, I agree. Bad enough for Emerson to try to force you out like he has. But it's still a jump to blame Singer for Emily. I get that the initial attack on Emily was similar to what he did to Martha, but unfortunately, drugging an intended victim at a party or restaurant is pretty common. And Upton's pretty much admitted to being the initial assailant. He even signed the nondisclosure agreement, not only resigning his position but also giving up his rights to further develop his work with Singer, which could be worth a bundle. Why would he have done that if he wasn't guilty?"

"Maybe just to get out of here and put this mess behind him. Once he was accused of rape and murder, how could he stay? Better for him to take a job at Berkeley and get away from all this."

Karen frowned. "All right, I can see that. Let's walk through what you think happened."

"Okay, I had some time to think this through on the plane. Starting from the beginning, Singer was there at the restaurant to spike Emily's drink. If it wasn't Upton, then Singer's the only one who had an opportunity to drug her. And he could have used this delay-send thing on his email to establish what looked like a convincing alibi."

"So you think that Singer went up to his office after he dropped Upton off that night, let himself be seen by his students, and set up a bunch of emails to be sent off at later times over the next hour and a half? Then he went back to Emily's, assaulted her, and had time to go back to his office and be seen again by one of the students when he was leaving?"

"Right. It was the emails that convinced you he was in his office. Could you have seen on the server that they were written first and sent later?"

"No, the server just gives me the time they were actually sent. So that would have worked. But Singer's the one who brought the case to your attention in the first place. Why would he have done that if he was the guilty party?"

"That's the part that bothered me the most, until I realized this wasn't just an ordinary assault. Singer had dual motives. Sure, he raped Emily for whatever sick reasons he has for attacking women. But he also wanted to frame Upton for it."

Karen looked puzzled. "I don't get it. Why would he want to do that? They were collaborators on an important research project."

"That's precisely why. His plan was to discredit Upton and take over the project for himself. Remember how insistent he was on getting Upton to relinquish his rights to further development of their drug? Singer didn't want to share the credit for their work with Upton. He wanted it all for himself."

Karen looked up at the ceiling and shook her head. "Yes, he definitely wanted that as part of the nondisclosure agreement. You really think he set this all up and raped Emily for scientific credit? What a piece of shit."

"I'm afraid that's exactly what I think. He drugged Emily in the restaurant and then went back to Emily's apartment and assaulted her after Upton left. Which fits what the woman with the dog said about seeing a big man outside that night. It wasn't the ex-boyfriend. It was Singer. The only thing I don't get is how he got into Emily's apartment."

"That'd be easy enough," Karen said. "Picking the kind of lock she had is trivial. All you need is a credit card. You can even find some nice instructional videos on the web."

"Okay, so he had the whole thing planned out. It helped that Emily texted her friend Carol, but I figure he would have come to me with the accusations even if she hadn't. You remember how he told us he was suspicious of Upton that night anyway."

"Yes, just because of the way Upton acted. And he counted on Emily knowing that something had happened, so one way or another we'd have gotten the story out of her."

"And nailed Upton for it. As long as Emily couldn't identify her assailant, pinning it on Upton by coming to me was straightforward."

Karen sighed. "Yes, we all believed it. You're the only one who had any doubts."

"Just vague misgivings. It all would have worked out like Singer planned, but then Emily started to remember."

"And Singer was right there in the dean's office when I got the call that things were coming back to her," Karen said. "Once that happened, he had to kill her to protect himself. Like we thought Upton did."

"Yes, that's what I think happened. And he used the same email alibi for the night she was killed."

Karen nodded. "It all makes sense. I think you're right. But now the question is how to prove it. We're not going to get anywhere with what we have at this point, especially given President Emerson's support of the bastard."

"I'm pretty sure that Linda, the woman in Wisconsin, will talk to the police."

"Maybe," Karen said. "But her story's just hearsay about something that happened ten years ago. Even if they believe her, she doesn't have anything that links Singer to Emily."

I got up and started pacing. "Is there any way your computer guys could see if he actually used this delay-send thing?"

"They might be able to if they could get hold of his computer for forensic analysis. But I don't think we'll be able to do that without some kind of direct evidence, especially if he's being protected by Emerson. I'm afraid we're going to have to somehow catch him in the act. Hopefully before he goes on to attack anyone else."

"Huh!" I scoffed. "Catch him in the act of what, assaulting another student? How the hell do you expect to do that?"

She smiled. But it wasn't the warm smile that I loved about her. This was the way a snake might smile at a mouse before turning it into dinner. "Not to worry. I have a plan."

My eyes widened. "A plan?"

"I'm afraid you're not going to like it," she said. "But you have a part to play. You better sit back down while I explain."

I sat down and listened. And I objected more than once. As strenuously as I could. But she was determined, and maybe she was right. Maybe this was the only way.

She was certainly right that I didn't like it.

27

I waited until late afternoon to call Westman and tell him that I'd accept his offer. I said that all I wanted now was to get out with some chance of finding another job elsewhere. I'd be more than happy to never hear about Mike Singer again. He told me that I'd made a wise choice, and he'd have the paperwork ready tomorrow. Once I signed, the charges would be dropped.

Two hours later, I headed over to Singer's office. I got there a little before five thirty. We'd changed back from daylight saving time a few days ago, so it was already dark.

Singer was alone, working on his computer. I knocked on the open door and went in, closing it behind me.

His eyes widened when he saw me. "What're you doing here? I was told you'd been banned from campus."

He started to reach for his phone, but I held up my hands. "It's okay—don't worry. I've accepted an offer to resign, on the condition that I keep my mouth shut. I'll sign and be gone tomorrow, but I wanted to warn you first."

His eyes narrowed as he looked at me. "Warn me? What are you talking about?"

"Look, I'm done with this. Out of here tomorrow. I know you've figured out that I pried into what happened at Yale. I was only trying to track down the missing grant money. I never thought it would end up tying in with Emily's case. It doesn't matter anymore anyway. Hell, it was years ago. I wish I'd never found out in the first place, but it's finished. And my lips are sealed."

He stared at me silently. I wondered if he knew I was lying. Finally, he shrugged. "So why come here? Westman already told me things were settled."

"It's that detective woman I worked with. You remember, we interviewed you together?"

"I remember. Reynolds or something like that, right?"

"Richmond. Karen Richmond," I said. "Anyway, she's like a bulldog, and she thinks you're the one who raped Emily. And maybe even murdered her."

His expression didn't change. "Why would she think that?"

"I don't know, based on what happened at Yale, I guess. And she said Emily told her something that puts the blame on you for her initial assault."

"What the hell's that supposed to mean?"

"Look, I don't know what she has or doesn't have. The point is, she's still pursuing this, and I don't want to be blamed for what she does. I told her about Yale before I agreed to keep quiet, and I think she's nuts for thinking you're responsible for Emily. But she does, and she's going after you."

Maybe it was my imagination, but he seemed to blink just a little more rapidly. "You say she's pursuing this crazy notion. What's she planning to do?"

"That's why I came over here, to warn you. She's put together a case and is going to file charges against you. I just talked to her, and she's in her office now. Maybe you can talk her out of it. Or get Westman to deal with her."

He got up from his chair. "All right, thanks for the warning. I'll see what I can do. Let's just keep this between the two of us, okay?"

"No problem," I said. "I don't want to have anything else to do with this."

I extended my hand, and he shook it. His palms were sweaty.

I turned left when I exited the building and walked a block down to my car. It was pointing away from the building, but with a good view of the entrance from the side mirror. I checked the view, adjusted the mirror, and called Karen.

"I think he bought it," I said. "He was so nervous that it felt like I was shaking hands with a wet dish towel when I left."

She chuckled. "Good for you for shaking hands with him. You couldn't have enjoyed that little ritual."

"Anything for the cause. So now I'm in my car, a block to the west. With a clear view of the entrance in my mirror."

"Good. Call me again when he leaves."

It didn't take long. Ten minutes later, I saw Singer exit the building and turn east, in the direction of Karen's office.

I called and reported, "He's on the move. Heading toward you."

"Okay. Wait a few minutes and then circle around so you come in from the opposite direction. See if he sets up outside my building."

I gave him a five-minute head start. Then I made a three-block circle and stopped a safe distance before reaching Karen's building, headed west. I could see a large figure waiting by the entrance, so I doused the lights and called Karen again.

"Someone's waiting outside. I can't see who it is in the dark, but it looks like a big man. Could be Singer."

"That's good enough. Don't try to get any closer. It's not worth the risk of your being spotted. Are you ready to move out?"

This was the part I really, really didn't like. I'd tried to talk her out of it but failed. And rationally, I knew she was right. But I couldn't stop myself from taking one more shot.

"Look, this is just too risky. Why don't we call the cops and let them pick him up? He was a nervous wreck when I left him. He'll break under questioning."

"Brad, c'mon. We've been over and over this." She made no attempt to disguise the impatience in her voice. "He's not going to break and confess to rape and murder. This is the only way to nail him. And I need you to back me up. Are you with me or not?"

What could I say? "All right, all right. Of course, I'm with you."

"Good. Just hang tough, and we'll nail the bastard. He's not going to hurt me. I'm expecting him, and I've got pepper spray and my gun, if I need it. It's not like I'm Emily, walking home unsuspecting."

"I know. It's just that I care about you, and he's a scary bastard. But I know you can handle it." At least I thought I believed that, even if the butterflies in my stomach were unconvinced.

"Let's get going, then. Are you ready?"

"Yes, I'm following your phone on the tracking app now."

"Okay. And you have your earbuds?"

I put them in. "Yep."

"All right. Get yourself in position along the parallel track we outlined, and call me when you're ready. After that, we'll keep the phone line open, and I'll be in constant communication."

I got out of the car and walked north, a block away from the route Karen was going to take. My job was to stay parallel to Karen's course, far enough away that Singer couldn't spot me but close enough to get to her quickly when needed.

If he took the bait.

When I got to the appointed corner, I called again. "Okay, I'm here."

"Leaving now," she said. "Keep the line open and follow me on the phone."

A few minutes later, I saw her phone leave the building and turn right. "Spotted him at the entrance," she said. "Moving out."

Every fiber of my being wanted to stop this. Karen using herself as bait to catch a killer! All I had to do was to go to her instead of following the plan. Let someone else catch Singer. But I couldn't. I had to do what I'd said I would. So I kept my eyes on the phone and followed a block away.

Two blocks later, Karen said, "Turning down the alley."

I clenched my teeth and said, "Okay." This was a diversion planned to give Singer the perfect opportunity for an attack. A deserted dark alley, much like the place where Emily had been killed.

She was a few minutes into it when she said, "It's deserted, except someone just turned in after me. A large man."

My heart leaped. "I'm coming to you."

Her voice was tense. "Okay, but go slow and keep some distance. I don't want him to see you. I've got the pepper spray ready."

I started moving toward her.

Suddenly I heard her yell, "Hold it, police!"

Then there were sounds of a scuffle, followed by a scream.

I was running full speed, heart pounding, when she cried out, "Got the bastard!"

He was on his stomach when I turned the corner into the alley, writhing from the pepper spray. Karen had her knee firmly planted on his neck and was cuffing his hands behind his back.

"Thank God you're okay," I gasped.

She raised her head. "I'm just fine," she said. "This couldn't have worked better. We've got him now."

She got up and turned him over with her foot. His eyes were closed, and he was helplessly coughing and sputtering. Just as it should be.

Except that it wasn't Mike Singer.

28

"Shit!" Karen swore. "Just some random son of a bitch who thought I was an easy mark. We caught the wrong damn fish." She kicked her would-be assailant in frustration.

I tried for a bit of levity. "Maybe the bait was too attractive to resist."

She gave a grim laugh. "Oh, shut up. This jerk was probably just after my bag. And if Singer *was* following me, he's gone now."

"So what do we do?"

"I'm going to call for backup and take this piece of crap into the station." She nudged him with her foot again for emphasis. "I'll have to go in with them to make a report and file charges. Why don't you go home, and I'll come over when I'm done? Maybe an hour or two. We're going to have to come up with an alternate plan."

I waited with Karen until the backup came. Neither of us said much—we were alone with our thoughts. I couldn't read her mind, but I suspected it was running pretty much along the same track as mine. *If this had been our best shot at getting Singer, what were we going to do next?* I hoped she was having better luck at finding an answer than I was.

It took maybe ten frustrating minutes for two cruisers to show up and pull into the head of the alley, blue lights flashing. They put Karen's assailant in one car, and Karen got into the other. I watched them take off and started to walk home, the same unanswered question bouncing around my head.

By the time I got home, I was in a real funk. Karen and I were both out of our jobs, and my career was in shambles. Maybe I should sign the damned agreement—the two of us could just go hide somewhere. A cabin in New Hampshire. Or a nice island in the Caribbean. True, running away didn't satisfy my sense of justice. But we could always shoot Singer before skipping town.

I went straight to the kitchen and poured a glass of scotch when I got home. A large one—I needed lots of inspiration. I took an initial sip and then a larger swallow. Maybe it would help.

Rosie was jumping up and down at my feet, so I turned around to pet her. Instead I recoiled in shock, the drink falling from my hand.

Mike Singer was sitting in my favorite chair by the window, holding a gun pointed at my chest. He let out a sarcastic snort. "Surprised to see me? Did you really think I was going to fall for your stupid trap?"

I grabbed the counter and took a deep breath to fight down the panic. My only chance was to connect with him. Get him talking. Get close to him and go for the gun.

"Mike, c'mon. What are you talking about? I told you I was done with everything. How'd you get in here, anyway?"

"Easy. All it took was a credit card with that wimpy lock you have." He motioned with the gun to a chair at the dining table.

"Sit down over there and we'll talk. Pour yourself another drink first. We're going to chat for a bit."

I refilled my glass and took the seat he indicated. Any opportunity to stall until I had an opening was worth taking.

Rosie came over and rubbed against me, looking puzzled. I knew she sensed my anxiety and wanted to help. Too bad she wasn't a German shepherd—a pug wasn't much use as an attack dog.

"Actually, your little trap was a pretty good ploy," Singer said. "I followed your detective friend and was about to jump her in the alley. Until someone else beat me to it."

So it had almost worked. But still, what did he really know? I had to convince him that he wasn't in danger. Give him a way out that didn't require shooting me.

"I don't know what you're talking about," I said. "What trap?"

He laughed. A short, scornful sound. "Don't play me for a fool. I saw you in the alley with her. Complaining that your victim wasn't me."

So much for that. "All right, fine. We did try to trap you. I told you before, Karen suspected you of the murder. But now she doesn't have any way to prove it. You can just walk out of here at this point with no harm done. Why get yourself in more trouble?"

"Sorry, but I don't think so. Not with the two of you left alive to keep after me."

I took another pull at the scotch. "Killing us isn't going to help you. Karen's a detective. She's told her whole unit about her suspicions."

He made the sarcastic laughing sound again. "You really must think I'm dumb. If that was true, she would've had real cops for backup in the alley. Not just you."

"They didn't know she was going to pull the alley trick. She said they wouldn't let her if she told them. Too dangerous. She organized it with me on her own."

"Yeah, sure she did." He raised the gun so that it pointed at my head. "Enough of your stupid bullshit. This'll end with the two of you. I have a nice suicide planned for you. Your note's already written. Sad how you were too despondent over your arrest and the end of your career to go on. And your detective friend will be another rape and murder victim, just like you tried to set up. Except it'll happen later tonight when she's not expecting me."

"Who are you kidding?" I said. "You can't fake a suicide by shooting me."

He grinned. "Sure I can. You'll pass out in a few more minutes from the ketamine I added to your scotch. The whole department knows having a glass of scotch is what you do when you get home, so that was an easy setup. Once you're out, I'll help you hold the gun to your head, and your own finger will pull the trigger. Your prints on the gun, powder burns on your hands, a nice note left behind for the cops. Nobody'll think twice about it."

I had only one move left, and I didn't know how long it would be before the drug hit me. Maybe just a few more minutes. Playing to his ego seemed like my best shot.

I let out a sigh. "I guess I should've known you'd have it all figured out. Pretty much the same way you drugged Emily, right? And the woman back in New Haven?"

"Yep, and others before them," he said. "But Emily had a dual purpose."

"Because you used her to frame Upton and push him out of future work on the drug?"

"Maybe you're not as stupid as I thought," he said. "I deserved credit for Immunoboost, not that little jerk. Now it's all mine. And it would have worked perfectly until Emily started to remember what happened."

I felt dizzy, and I could tell my speech was starting to slur. The drug was kicking in. But I had to stay focused. He was getting more and more absorbed in himself. It would be time soon.

I picked up my glass. "So you attacked her a second time? And killed her."

"That was unfortunate, but I didn't have any choice. She could have ruined everything."

The time might or might not have been right, but I couldn't hold off any longer. I threw my glass at his face and jumped up to charge him. A last chance to grab for the gun.

Except my legs collapsed, and I fell to the floor. I'd waited too long.

"Nice try," he said. "Looks like it's time now."

I watched helplessly as he approached me. I could barely move, and my vision was blurred.

I sensed some kind of movement to the side.

Then I heard the gun go off.

And everything went black.

29

My head was pounding, and the ceiling was spinning. At least I thought it was the ceiling, although I couldn't see clearly. I tried to roll over, and someone started to run toward me. Singer? But hadn't he already shot me?

I started to yell, but whoever it was gently took my head in warm hands. A soft voice said, "Shh, it's all right. You're okay now."

I managed to focus. And saw Karen kneeling beside me. "Take it easy. Don't try to move yet," she said.

A wave of relief swept over me. "Karen? How did you get here? Where's Singer?" I forced myself to a sitting position and started to look around the apartment. Nobody there but Karen. And Rosie, who was vigorously snuggling up to me.

"Singer's all taken care of," she said. "I got here just in time, while you had him talking. I could hear him as soon as I opened the door, so I snuck in quietly, and neither of you saw me. Then you threw the glass at him, and I had my chance to jump him with the pepper spray. The gun went off and put a hole in the wall, but that was it. You'll be fine as soon as the drug wears off."

I squeezed her hand. "Did you hear what he was saying? I can't remember exactly, but I think he was talking about killing Emily."

"I heard him, and it'll probably come back to you too. But even better, it'll all be recorded on Rosie's surveillance system. Thanks to you being such a goofy dog owner, we have his full confession on tape."

Relief washed over me. It had worked after all. I rubbed Rosie's head to thank her for getting us the recording system. "So where is he now?" I asked.

"I called for help, and they've taken him downtown. You've been out for over an hour. They'll want to get a statement from you, but it can wait until tomorrow. Maybe you'll be able to remember more then, but it really doesn't matter. We have plenty to be sure that he spends the rest of his life in a cage."

"So it's really over? You have enough to put him away?"

She smiled again. But this time, there was a cold look in her eyes. "Singer's finished. But it's not quite over yet. You and I still have a bit more work to do."

The room had gone back to spinning in my head. "Now?" I asked.

She bent over and kissed me. "No. After you get some sleep and you're back to being yourself again."

———

I was naked in bed when I woke up. I didn't remember getting here, but I did remember Singer trying to kill me last night. And Karen saving my ass.

I threw on a robe and padded out to the kitchen. Karen was there with a cup of coffee and a newspaper in front of her.

"Good to see you walking on your own," she said. "Get some coffee and take a look at this."

Most of the front page of the *Globe* was devoted to Singer's arrest. Karen was the woman of the hour, the heroic detective who'd single-handedly taken down a monster—dubbed the "College Killer" by the reporter. I got a sidebar mention as her helper and near next victim, which was plenty for me.

"How'd they get all this?" I asked.

"The chief called them as soon as we arrested Singer last night. He loves publicity for the department, even if it was about me instead of him. Anyway, the news people were all over it. I spent an hour or so with a reporter after I got you to bed, and he hustled to get it in this morning's paper. And of course, it was immediately picked up by TV and radio, so it's all over the place now."

I swallowed more coffee. It felt great going down. "So you're the star of the hour. Maybe even of the day—or week. They're not going to fire you after this, I assume."

"No, they already offered me a promotion instead." She shrugged. "Not sure if I want it, though. The chief's still the same. Anyway, I'll see. First, we have some more work to do if you're up to it."

I finished the coffee and stood up. "A quick shower and I'll be good to go. Where to?"

"You'll see. Don't worry—it's an errand you'll enjoy."

———

We got to the Presidential Palace a little before nine. It was still an impressive building, but it seemed to have lost much of its grandeur since my last visit. Perhaps because I knew it was about to take a fall. Or at least the man at the top was.

Two uniforms met us outside, but Karen asked them to wait in the lobby while we took the elevator up to the top floor. The receptionist greeted us with an icy stare.

"Do you have an appointment?" she asked.

"No," Karen said. "But I think President Emerson may be expecting us." She held up her badge.

The receptionist glanced at it but was unimpressed. "I'm sorry, but nobody just walks in to see the president." She pushed a button on the desk, and two well-muscled apes in black suits appeared from nowhere. "Please see these two out," she said.

One of them grabbed Karen's arm, and I half expected her to pepper spray him. But instead she said, "Don't you recognize me?"

"From where, the local nuthouse? C'mon, lady, let's go."

"I was thinking you might have seen this morning's news."

He paused, and a look of recognition crossed his face. "Wait, are you the one who took down that rapist?"

She nodded. "That's me. And do you want to be the cop who threw me out of the building? Our new chief will love that."

He let go of her arm and seemed to be trying to think. Then he turned to the receptionist. "Sorry, Alice, let them go ahead in."

Karen said, "You can stay where you are, Alice. We'll let ourselves in."

And we proceeded into President Emerson's inner sanctum.

He was sitting behind his big desk with a copy of the *Globe* in front of him. Our entrance startled him, and he looked up sharply. "What's this about?"

"It's about obstruction of justice," Karen said. "Kenneth Emerson, I'm placing you under arrest."

"You're crazy," he spat. "You can't do that! You work for the institute. For me."

"I'm a police officer, sworn to enforce the law. That comes before loyalty to whoever signs my paycheck."

He stared at us, and a moment passed as he got control of himself. I could almost picture the gears in his head shifting as his face morphed into the picture of the prototypical college president. A pleasant, reasonable man.

Maybe he'd offer us tea.

"Of course, I understand your priorities," he said. "But I have no idea what you're talking about. Obstruction of justice? Whatever you're thinking, I'm sure I can explain."

"We're talking about rape and murder," Karen said. "And Michael Singer."

He sighed audibly and shifted his eyes to include me in his response. "All right, I know you've dug into the nondisclosure agreement I signed with Singer at Yale. But that's standard academic practice to get rid of a tenured faculty member who's gotten into trouble. Your dean did the same with Steve Upton."

I couldn't contain myself any longer. "And then you continued supporting Singer here, where he's raped and murdered one of our students. Was that a little tit for tat after he helped you get the president's job?"

"Look, I tried to explain this to you before," Emerson said. "Singer was one of our top faculty members. He brought in more grant money than anyone else, and with this new Immunoboost thing, he would've made us the top research institute in the country. Supporting him was a no-brainer."

"A known rapist?" Karen said. "And when he did the same and worse here, you tried to protect him by framing Brad and having him arrested. He was part of an ongoing investigation that you attempted to obstruct."

"Wait a minute," Emerson said. "I don't know anything about Brad's arrest. Are you saying it was some kind of setup? If that's true, I'll be happy to deal with the responsible parties. Most severely, I can assure you."

"The responsible party is Doug Westman," Karen said. "Acting on your orders. He gave up the whole story to our detectives last night."

Emerson snorted and raised his eyebrows. "And all you have is his word for that? I don't know why he would have done such a crazy thing. Maybe he thought it would please me. But we never talked about it." He laughed. "And now Westman's trying to make a deal to save his own ass. That'll never hold up in court. My lawyers will get it thrown out so fast your heads will spin."

Karen smiled at him. "You might get off in court. We'll see. But it's not going to matter after I'm through with you. This is going to be sort of the opposite of a nondisclosure agreement. Now stand up and put your hands out. I'll be nice enough to cuff you in front if you cooperate."

He paled when he saw Karen take out the cuffs, but he stood up. "You don't have to handcuff me. I'll go with you."

Karen grabbed his right arm and snapped the cuffs on. I grabbed his left and held it out for her to do the same. "Hope you don't mind a little help," I said.

"Not at all. Would you like to walk out with us?"

"Always happy to assist an officer of the law."

Emerson was squirming as we perp walked him out of his office, Karen on his right and me on his left. Alice was still at her reception desk. Her mouth dropped to the floor when she saw us. Emerson yelled at her to call his lawyer, but she seemed too shocked to move.

Other staffers had the same reaction as we dragged him to the elevator, with Emerson yelling that they'd better not say anything about this to anyone.

The lobby was empty when we got to the ground floor, having been cleared by the two uniformed cops who were standing at the front door. It was when we opened that door that all hell broke loose. We were greeted by three squad cars and news trucks from some half a dozen local television stations. Not to mention a crowd of reporters and photographers all yelling for attention. And a growing throng of interested bystanders.

Emerson tried to hide his face from the cameras as we strong-armed him through the crowd, but his efforts to cover his face only accentuated the handcuffs. In the meantime, Karen answered a few of the reporters' questions.

Her simple statement, "Kenneth Emerson is under arrest for obstruction of justice in the case of Michael Singer," elicited a frantic scrambling and jostling of video cams, microphones, and smartphones.

One reporter shouted, "Isn't Singer the man who was arrested last night?"

"The murderer and rapist I arrested last night," Karen clarified. "And now we're bringing the man who made Singer's crimes possible to justice as well."

"How did President Emerson do that?" another reporter yelled.

"I can't provide further details at this time," Karen said.

When we finally got Emerson into the back seat of a squad car, I was pretty sure he understood what Karen had done to him. But just to make it clear, she drove the stake home. "Check out the news later today. I bet they somehow get the full story."

His eyes had the frantic look of a cornered animal when the car pulled away.

30

The campus went crazy following Emerson's arrest. The news media were all over the place, looking under all the rocks for anything they could dig up. As soon as the early reports came out, a crowd of angry students and quite a few faculty members took over the Presidential Palace in a massive protest, demanding Emerson's immediate dismissal. The board of trustees initially put him on paid leave pending resolution of the charges against him, but that wasn't good enough for the mob. They were screaming for immediate blood—nothing less than his resignation.

Somehow the *Globe* got the full story, and it was all over the TV and internet by that afternoon. The initial report attributed it to "an anonymous but highly placed source." Karen just gave me a knowing wink when I asked her about it. Anyway, that sealed Emerson's fate. The trustees called another emergency meeting and voted to fire him by the end of the day. Not even a chance to resign.

The *Globe* story described the roles Karen and I had played, so the news pack was after us. We decided to get out of Dodge and avoid more publicity by spending a few days at the inn we'd stayed at in New Hampshire. It seemed like ages ago.

Neither of us answered our phones or responded to emails, and we had three idyllic days of relaxing, eating, and making love. Rosie enjoyed the relaxing and eating and was at least willing to tolerate the sex. I could have gone on forever, but the reporters somehow found us. When I got up and looked out the window on the morning of day four, I was greeted by the unwelcome sight of news trucks and reporters milling about in the parking lot. I guess we had become celebrities.

I closed the shades before they spotted me and went back to bed with the bad news. Karen put a positive spin on it. "Time to sneak out of here," she said. "Anyway, we have more work to do."

"I'm all for sneaking out and getting away from these jerks. But what do you mean more work? I know a nice place up in Maine where we could hide out instead of here. Rosie'd be welcome, and we can keep on doing what we've been doing."

I ran my hand down her naked back to accentuate the advantages of what we were doing. She smiled and stretched like a cat. "I like what we're doing too. But you don't want to let Sally Lipton get away with her role in this, do you?"

I hadn't thought much about Sally Lipton since returning from Madison. But Karen was right. "No, I guess I don't," I admitted. "Her signing the nondisclosure agreement enabled Singer to get away with it in New Haven. In a way, she was as guilty there as Emerson."

"Exactly," Karen said. "And it's even worse for a woman to help a rapist hide his crimes. She needs to pay for it."

"But how? You don't have anything to charge her with—not like the way you went after Emerson."

"No, she hasn't committed any crime. At least not that we know about. But think, why did she sign the nondisclosure agreement?"

"Two reasons, I suppose. The first was that she wasn't going to get tenure, and Emerson offered her a research faculty position as a fallback. That's unheard of at a top university and against all standard practice at Yale, where she would normally have had to leave if she failed to get tenure. Up or out. But Emerson broke all the rules to buy her off and let her stay."

"And the second was the money Singer paid her, right? The ongoing consulting fees that put you onto this in the first place."

"Correct. Although I bet the job was more important," I said. "Singer probably just kept up the payments to make sure she stayed on the hook."

"So how do you think we should take care of her?" Karen had an enigmatic look in her eyes. A look that I could tell meant trouble for somebody.

I tried for the same look in return, even though I didn't think I could pull it off. "We take the job away from her."

"Exactly," Karen said. "Can your friend down there give us a hand? We need to have an authority figure from the university with us when we confront her."

"I'll give Martin a call," I said. "Should we get out of here first?"

By a lucky coincidence, we'd parked by a side entrance that wasn't visible from the main parking lot. Within fifteen minutes, we gathered up our stuff and made it to the car without being spotted. No showers, not even breakfast and a walk for Rosie, until we were safely away from the inn via back roads to the highway. Then we found a rest stop where Karen and I could grab coffee and Rosie could eat and use the outdoor facilities.

After that, Karen drove while I worked the phone to make the necessary arrangements. A few hours later, we checked into a hotel in New Haven, with time to shower and put on fresh clothes before meeting Martin.

A woman was waiting for us with Martin when we got to his office. Martin introduced her as Eleanor Stoker, chair of chemistry, which was Sally Lipton's department. She was young for a department chair, maybe early forties, but her solemn face and piercing brown eyes left no doubt as to her authority. She held up an envelope and said, "Martin thought I should come with you, okay? If Lipton's done what you say, I want her out. Immediately."

Without waiting for an answer, she led the way out of Martin's office. Once we were in the hall, two security guards swung in behind us and followed us to Lipton's office in the Chemistry Research Building. The door was closed, but that didn't slow Eleanor down. She barged in on Lipton talking to a young man, presumably a student, and unceremoniously said, "Get out."

The fire in her eyes brooked no delay, and he gathered his things and left as Karen, Martin, and I followed her in. The security guards waited outside. They seemed to know how this was going to go down.

Lipton wasn't as cowed as the student and tried for her usual snobbish dismissiveness. "What's this about? That was my research assistant. We have work to do."

"Not anymore, you don't." Eleanor handed her the letter. "Your employment at Yale University is immediately terminated with cause."

Lipton jumped out of her chair. "What the hell are you talking about! You can't do this."

"I can and I have." Eleanor inclined her head to Karen. "Would you like to explain it to her?"

Karen looked at Lipton as if she'd like to tear her apart with her bare hands. It was enough to make Lipton shrink back and abandon her posture of aggression. "You've covered up Michael Singer's crimes ever since he raped Martha Daniels ten years ago at a party at your house. You protected him from the consequences of that by signing a nondisclosure agreement that Kenneth Emerson organized, and you've maintained your silence while he raped and murdered another student at BTI. Not to mention your culpability for Martha Daniels's suicide."

Lipton turned pale and tried to say something, but Karen continued. "And all for what? A lousy position as a research faculty member when you weren't good enough to get tenure. And some payoff money from Singer. Well, the money's over. Singer and Emerson are finished."

Then Eleanor had the last word. "And so is your position here. And you should be aware that your file will state the grounds for your dismissal, so don't harbor any hopes of finding another job somewhere else." She opened the door, and the security guards came in. "These gentlemen will escort you off campus. Do not return. Your personal belongings will be mailed to your home address. Now get the hell out of my department!"

Lipton was trembling and in tears by the time Eleanor finished. She let the security guards lead her away without further protest.

When she was gone, Eleanor turned to us. "Thank you for ridding my department of that scum." Then she turned and left.

We were silent for a moment. Finally, Karen spoke. "She's a good woman."

"Yes, there was no doubt in her mind about what had to be done," Martin said. "Are the two of you satisfied?"

"We would have preferred jail," I said. "But we really didn't have evidence for criminal charges. And this destroys her professionally. Since her career was her reason for doing what she did, at least the punishment fits the crime."

"Yes, it's fitting," Karen added. Turning to Martin, she said, "Thank you for your help. Brad's told me how you were with him in this from the beginning."

Martin smiled. "No need to thank me. Just meet me at L'Auberge at seven. New Haven's best restaurant. And Brad, bring your wallet."

He and I both laughed, a mixture of amusement and the release of tension. When he left, Karen asked what that was all about.

"You'll see," I said. "The man does anything and everything for food."

———

L'Auberge looked like it was up to Martin's billing. The rich, wood-paneled walls, crystal chandeliers, and tables set with sparkling silver and elegant china all spelled fine dining. We were seated at a corner table next to a large window with a view of the Yale campus and the Kline Biology Tower. An appropriate setting.

When the server came over, Martin waved away the menus. "We'll all have the eight-course tasting menu," he announced. "And a bottle of your best champagne to start, the Cristal. That's okay with you two, right?"

I looked at Karen, and she laughed. "Sure. Sounds like there'll be plenty left to take home to Rosie." I could tell she was enjoying Martin in his favorite role as head gourmand.

When the champagne came, Martin raised his glass. "To the two of you." We clinked glasses, and he said, "You're quite a pair. Between you, you've brought down a rapist and a murderer, not to mention the president of a major university. What's next?"

Karen smiled. "Well, at this point we've both lost our jobs at BTI, so I guess we're free agents."

Martin chuckled. "You know that'll be reversed. Brad, what do you want to do next? BTI is going to be looking for a new president."

"No, the board of trustees moved quickly for once and offered the presidency to my dean. Or maybe I should say drafted her into the position. Anyway, she'll be good. One of the first things she did was to sign over all the rights to Immunoboost to Steve Upton, so he'll be able to pursue whatever's going to come from that project."

"Too bad you couldn't keep him at BTI," Martin said.

"No chance of that," I said. "Not after what he went through. In fact, there was talk about his suing us. But he's happy with his new job at Berkeley, and giving him the Immunoboost rights put a stop to the threat of legal action."

The first course arrived with a flourish. Poached Maine lobster with roasted strawberries and an array of accompaniments. Martin tasted it and sat back with a look of pure joy.

"Ahh, perfection. Well, maybe you'll be the new dean, then."

I shook my head. "I'm sure you mean that kindly, but I've had enough of the upper reaches of university politics. I'll finish up my stint as department chair and then get back to the lab. That's why I got into this in the first place."

Martin nodded. "I remember your telling me that one of your students had something good going. That should help get your research back in gear."

I winked at Karen, remembering how much trouble that had caused.

"Ironically, it's a collaboration my student started with one of Steve Upton's," I explained to Martin. "Which we'll continue, although it'll be a cross-country endeavor now."

Karen squeezed my hand under the table.

"Funny how things work out," Martin said. "How about you, Karen? Going to stay at BTI or go off and become chief of your own department somewhere? You're duly famous as Boston's finest now."

Karen looked thoughtful. And I wanted to hear the answer to that one myself. It was a question that made me nervous. And one we hadn't talked about since she mentioned the job offer she'd gotten from Chicago.

Finally, she said, "To tell you the truth, I'm not sure. I may look around a bit."

My stomach fell. Until she reached over and put her hand on my arm. "But it'll be in Boston, with Brad."

I liked that—it had a good ring to it. We clinked glasses again as Martin signaled for more champagne.

ACKNOWLEDGMENTS

It's a pleasure to thank Florence Haseltine (executive director of Health Research, University of Texas at Arlington, and founder of the Society for Women's Health Research) for a discussion of sexual harassment at the beginning of this project. Some of her thoughts helped Brad figure out what was going on!

I'm again grateful to my friends Alexandra and Ken Adams, who read and critiqued the manuscript. Especially Alexandra, who went through it more than once.

And special thanks to Audrey, Patti, and Beau for their patience, inspiration, and support.

ABOUT THE AUTHOR

Geoffrey M. Cooper is a retired scientist and academic administrator, having held positions at Harvard Medical School and Boston University as professor, department chair, and associate dean. He is the author of several scientific texts and is now using his experience in academic medicine as background for writing fiction. His debut novel was the award-winning medical thriller *The Prize*. He lives in Ogunquit, Maine.

Website: geofcooper.com

Reviews from readers are greatly appreciated. If you enjoyed *Nondisclosure*, please let other readers know by leaving your comments on Amazon or Goodreads.